CAPTIVE

A YA Dystopian Romance

K. A. Gandy

THIGPEN-GANDY PUBLISHING

THIGPEN-GANDY PUBLISHING

CONTENTS

CHAPTER ONE

TERROR

DEMY

Nothing makes sense. My body aches everywhere, the lights are fuzzy—no, my *head* is fuzzy—and there's so much noise. People are yelling. Why are they yelling in my bedroom? I want to bury my head under my pillow and hide.

Except—where am I? I keep my eyes screwed shut against the yellowish glow over my head and pat the bed, but it's too hard to be a bed. Carpet? Did I fall asleep on the floor? And is that—

My eyes fly open. There's a body next to me.

Nell.

She looks dead. Oh my God, is she dead? My hand fumbles as I reach for her. It lands clumsily against her neck, but I can feel a steady pulse under my fingertips. Thank God. *Thank God.*

"Hey, we got one moving!" The words sound far away, but I somehow know they're bad news. Who is that?

"Just stick her again. We've got a way to go yet."

Rough, calloused hands grab my chin and turn my head to the side, exposing my neck.

A sharp pinch of pain breaks through my haze for a few seconds, but then the all-consuming blackness returns, smothering my fear. Smothering me.

CHAPTER TWO

HONEY

DEMY

Consciousness comes back slowly, like thick honey oozing through my brain.

I need to find Nell. She was with me.

"Nell?" Her name comes out as a croak. "Nell, are you here?" My eyes wander.

The dirty, smudged white ceiling paint with chunks of old plaster hanging from above don't tell me where I am. I'm not entirely sure what happened, either—only that I'm cold. My fingers graze rough cement, and I realize I'm lying on the floor.

"Why are you on the floor, Demy?" I ask myself the question out loud, if for no reason other than to ground me. Something is very wrong, and I can tell I'm missing something. Something huge that I should know. But my head really hurts. My back is twisted, and knotted up like I slept wrong for a solid week.

Moving slowly, I lever myself up off the cold, gritty cement. The room I'm in isn't empty.

Another girl in a torn red party dress is sitting propped against the wall, but I don't recognize her.

"Demy, is it?" she asks, sounding bored. She's focused on straightening the tulle that pokes out from the bottom hem of the dress, not bothering to make eye contact.

"Yes. Where are we?"

"No idea. The Cabal took us."

Cabal? *Cabal.*

Oh, no. No, no, no. My memories burst through the slow-dripping sludge, assaulting me with painful clarity. Beckett's kiss. The boat ride, and the NLC guard who pulled the gun. Atlas was down, Nell was unconscious, and then they threw us in the back of a black SUV. Destination . . . this crappy place, apparently.

"Hey, you need to get a grip on yourself. If you hyperventilate you'll pass back out and whack your head." Her voice is cold, and there is no sympathy on her face. She smooths down the last section of material, and finally looks up at me.

It was better when she wasn't looking at me. Her eyes are bloodshot, nearly the color of the dress, and lifeless. There's nothing there but pure defeat, and I can't let that rub off on me. No.

My pulse pounds painfully in my temples as I breathe through my nose, trying to slow it down. She's right about one thing, at least; I can't afford to knock myself back out. I have to keep my head if I want any chance of getting out of here.

"Where are the others?" I ask when I can breathe almost normally.

She shrugs. "They don't keep us all together."

"What's your name?"

"Carla."

"How long have you been here, Carla?" I'm afraid of the answer, but I need it just the same.

She snorts. "Who knows? The months run together after a while."

I nod, biting my bottom lip. They have kept her alive, which is good. It means I'm not about to be brutally murdered, at least. I blow out another breath, and then get to my feet. My knees are shaking, but the need to inspect my prison is driving me harder than my physical limitations. I have no memory of my arms getting these deep scrapes, but since I woke up chucked on the ground like so much trash, it seems logical that the concrete took a piece out of me.

Cement block walls that used to be white line three sides, but the front . . . it's scuffed plexiglass. Ignoring my pounding head and skinned arms in favor of curiosity, I wobble closer to it.

"Don't do it. Stay back from there!" Carla is on her feet in a heartbeat, eyes wild as she grabs me by the shoulders and wrenches me away from the cloudy divider.

"What is wrong with you! How are we going to get out of here if we just stay in this box?" I try to yank away, my elbow smacking the plexi-glass with a painful *thwack*, but I'm still loose-limbed from whatever they drugged me with, and her grip is strong. Fingers like talons dig into my flesh, holding me captive. She drags me away from the front of our cell, her eyes wide and fearful as she shoves me roughly down against the back wall.

"Hey! What's going on in there?"

"No, you stupid idiot!" Carla's paranoid gaze lands on me as heavy footsteps come closer to the cell. "They're going to take *me*, and it's *your* fault." She tears at her stringy, unwashed hair with an anguished screech.

Well, she's gone off the deep end. How long has she been in here? The thought fills me with panic.

5

Her slap lands hard on my cheek, sending my head snapping to the side and making my already questionable senses go for a spin. My vision doubles, and I hang my head between my knees as my ears ring, leaving me utterly helpless.

But instead of attacking me further, she drops down next to me, and curls into a ball, covering her head with her arms.

The sound of something grating over concrete makes me want to look up, but I'm afraid if I do, I'll vomit all over myself and our cell.

Based on the stench in here . . . the last time that happened, it was never cleaned up. I swallow down the sour taste in my mouth, trying desperately not to make things any worse.

"You know the rules, Carla. No fighting." A smug masculine voice makes me risk moving to see our guard. The man is wearing a black cloak. His shaved head and cold smile complete the picture. I'm ashamed to say that I cower away from the man as he grabs Carla by the arm and drags her, screaming, from our cell. But when the grating sound comes again signaling that I'm alone in the cell, all I can do is weep.

A whole life of running, and the men who murdered my parents still caught me.

Chapter Three

HORROR

Fletcher

Two Days Earlier

Everything is going to hell. The attack alarms are blaring again, and I'm supposed to meet Demy any minute. I don't want to leave her here, but I also don't want to be the idiot who gets shot or captured because I stayed here on a bench like a sitting duck while the Cabal swarmed the NLC.

Indecision keeps me still. I don't see any signs of invaders, and I'm less than two minutes from the nearest safe room. If I see any sign of anyone besides Demy, I'll sprint for the safe room. It'll be tight, but I'll make it. Still, the grating alarms have me pushing to my feet, fighting the urge to pace.

Stay alert, stay sharp, I scold myself. I blow out a breath and run my hands through my hair. I left it down today, for my last planned date. And now, I'm cursing my vanity. It's a small thing, but I want to look nice for her. Want to convince her to pick me.

Which is wholly not what I expected, coming into this program. I expected to be matched, yes. I expected to find someone to start a family with. But Demy? She's nothing I ever saw coming. For a guy like me who's had every single thing in life handed to him, she's . . . a breath of fresh air. One I desperately need, even though I haven't *told* her that yet. I'm going to, today. Before I lose my nerve.

I scan the area again, tensing when I see someone running this way. My shoulders only relax a fraction when I realize it's Peter. He looks grim.

"Come with me!" He barks the order on the move, so I break into a run to keep up.

"What's going on?" I yell to be heard over the wailing alarms.

"There's been an attack. Three people were taken, and one is injured."

My heart stops dead in my chest before stuttering back to life. "Who is it?"

"I don't know yet. The injured person is being taken to the medical building."

"We're not going to the safe room?" I ask as we blow past it.

He shoots me a speculating look. "You can if you want to be locked down. But I'm heading for medical to get briefed. It's as secure as the safe rooms, assuming we get there in one piece."

"Let's go," I urge, and we pick up the speed into a full sprint.

My calves are burning and my sides are heaving, but we cut across the New Life Center grounds in record time. I drop one hand on my knee, watching our backs as Patrick punches in a code on the keypad. It beeps and then the door clicks open.

"Come on." Peter holds the door until I slip inside, then lets it seal behind us.

The medical building is one of the few I haven't been inside since I've been at the NLC. There's a tidy waiting room plastered with maternity photos and smiling babies, and a harried-looking receptionist wearing pink behind the desk.

"Are you two injured? The Medical building is in emergency lock down, so if you're healthy I'll need to re-route you to the nearest safe room."

"We're here with Pacelli Security for an update on the injured, and to speak with Atlas," Peter states, staring her down.

She wilts under his glare, but points to the double doors to the right. "They're through there. But there is already a representative here seeing to Mr. Pacelli. An . . . Easton?" she says, reading the name off her clipboard.

"So, Atlas is the one who's hurt?" My mind spins as I follow Peter through the swinging double doors, processing. I didn't bother to ask the man's last name before, so I'm assuming. "Who was he with, when they got him, if Easton is here and fine?"

"He was on a double date," Peter says, his expression grim as he looks at me, waiting for me to catch up.

Double date.

Atlas, Nell—no.

"Did they take Demy?" It's half question, half demand as I grab his arm, stopping him mid-stride.

He shakes me off with a glare. "I don't know yet, Fletcher. That's what we're here to find out. Whoever they took, we need to get them back, and quickly. The Cabal isn't kind to its victims."

Dread fills my veins like lead. Deep down, a part of me knows what I'm about to hear, even as we push into the only lit treatment room. Atlas is laid out flat on his back, a harried-looking doctor staring at beeping machinery while a nurse checks his vitals.

Easton stands off to the side, concern on his face as he listens to someone reporting over his comm.

"—no sign of any remaining Cabal on site. Requesting permission to rapid-follow."

He snaps orders into his comm. "Focus on securing the perimeter! We need to find any other breach points before we can pursue! I repeat, do not pursue off-property without approval!"

When he looks up at us, his expression is grave.

"What the hell happened?" Peter asks.

"They were at the pond; the posted guards were found tased and tied up. Atlas was alone with the women and Beckett when they attacked. Presumably, he put himself between the Cabal and the women, expecting backup. One of the NLC guards is missing, and the others—"

I don't need to hear the rest to know the truth, as I stare down at Atlas's prone form. Only one thing matters.

They've taken Demy, and I have to get her back.

Chapter Four

KNOCKOUT

Demy

Everything goes quiet again as soon as they close the door behind her, so now I'm in a near-silent box. There is nothing in the room but a toilet and sink behind a privacy screen, and a pair of single-width cots. The blankets smell sour when I finally manage to get back to my feet and flop myself down onto the closest cot, bringing the nausea roaring back to the forefront. I breathe through my mouth for a long time, begging it to pass.

It eventually does, but Carla doesn't come back.

When I fall asleep, I'm curled in a ball on top of the filthy bedding, alone and as small as I can make myself.

The scraping of the door wakes me. Sounds outside the cell are suddenly louder, startling me to awareness. Everything is clearer than it was the day before, which is a relief. I feel weak, but that could be the hollow emptiness of my stomach as much as the aftereffects of the knockout drugs.

I sit warily on my cot as the man pushes his way inside.

"On your feet."

Moving slowly, I do as he says. He's not the same man who took Carla away, though he's dressed identically, from the robe to the cold eyes. He's more bored than cruel, which I'll take as a good sign.

"Hurry up, I've got more girls to round up and I'm not getting chewed out because you're slow as dirt." He grabs me by the arm and tugs me from my cell. I keep quiet as I'm shoved into a line of women. Each of them is scruffy, in that "unwashed and unbrushed after a night out" sort of way. Some are crying, while others stare lifelessly at the wall. None of them is Nell, and fear inflates inside my chest like a balloon, blocking my lungs from inflating fully.

We stop at three more cells, and I barely contain a relieved sob when Nell is pulled from the last one. She's got an ugly bruise blossoming over her cheekbone and scratches along her forearms, but that familiar defiant tilt to her chin gives me hope. Hope of what, I don't know.

That we're both still fighting.

The guard herds us like so many sheep down the divided hallway, passing plenty of occupied cells. Another guard on the other side of the metal gate which splits the cell block herds his own line of women from the cells directly across from us. When we reach the end of the cell block, he uses a brass key to unlock it. I watch with rapt attention as he tucks the key back into a hidden pocket inside his cloak. I haven't seen a keyhole on my cell door, but from what I could see they are simple external latches. Which means once you're in, you can't get out without help.

Once we are out of the cell block, the space opens up, and I see dozens of people milling about at a central gathering area. Most of them are members of the Cabal, but there are women dressed in clothes of varying degrees of dishevelment mixed in, too. Most look fearful, but a few are draped languidly over the benches with the men, laughing or leaning hard into their sides. It's casual and haphazard, yet the sight still makes me shudder.

I don't have long to take in the scene because we're ushered through at a hurried clip, and falling behind even slightly earns me a cuff on the shoulder. I try to memorize the turns we take, but after the fifth one I lose count. My brain is still too foggy. We end the journey in a bleak-looking corridor. The door has blood streaks trailing away from the knob and the sight has me seeking out Nell, meeting her eyes with a worried gaze. She looks away quickly, so I do the same. When the door opens, a man in a white doctor's coat enters, his bald pate shining under the harsh overhead lights.

"How many this time?" the doctor asks, only barely looking up from his clipboard to acknowledge our existence.

"Fifteen," our captor answers.

"Bring them in. And stick around this time in case there are any issues."

The guard rolls his eyes at the doctor, but the guards follow us into the room nonetheless.

I let my eyes sink closed briefly, shutting out the world. I can't think about the women who came before me, who weren't saved. I can't do that, because if I do I'll lose my cool and, with it, any chance of escape. I suck in slow, deep breaths through my nose and then follow the line into the room.

It's a poor excuse for a medical facility; a drab, skinny room that must be a hundred feet long with a low ceiling, exam tables lining the entire back wall, threadbare curtains in between, and nothing but empty space for us to wait in like a herd of cattle. The sides of the room are lined with banks of medical equipment and cabinets holding supplies.

One of the girls starts crying as she's told to get on the table, but I do my best to block it out and focus on examining the treatment room for anything that could be used as a weapon. One by one, women are being taken to the tables as the guards creep closer to us from behind. Like wolves, dogging sheep. Instrument trays are haphazardly tossed on stands next to each one, but there's nothing there that is sharp enough for me to stab someone with. Gauze and medical tape won't get me far, and I have no idea what the blunted wand is for. Our orderly line has broken down, and no one seems to care which woman goes to which table, so I angle to the right, where there are more empty beds. Nell sees me and follows, staking a claim on the one between me and the wall.

A woman in scrubs with hard eyes and pasty skin walks down the line of exam tables, tossing tattered hospital gowns to us one by one.

"Strip and put this on. You're getting a full exam and a blood draw. If you fight, you will be restrained, and you don't want that." I catch the gown she gives me with one hand, and eye the men looming in front of the door. They don't have the decency to pull the curtains, or to look away. One is impassive, while the other leers in sick delight as the other girls start stripping down. Three more walk in and join Mr. Lascivious, and that's when I know it's hopeless. I couldn't fight my way past two, let alone five. An old, familiar numbness begins to steal into me, threatening to drag me under.

Nell is already moving, her motions wooden. She's turned her back on the men, and her shoulders are straight as she pulls the thin gown on before shrugging out of her jeans. She keeps her bra and underwear on, and when she's done she turns to me and mouths something.

Block it out.

I do my best to follow suit, keeping as much of myself covered as possible. I realize belatedly as I pull my shirt over my head and it catches, that I've still got one of my ruby earrings. I casually slip it free, and tuck it into the thigh pocket of my leggings before wadding them up. But it's not until the sounds of crying from multiple girls at the other side of the room reach me that I really start to go numb.

This is happening and there's nothing I can do to stop it. I eye the side table again, considering using the metal tray itself as a weapon. But even if I manage to fight my way past the doctor, nurse, and growing crowd of leering guards . . . I have nowhere to go, and no way out. Not to mention I'm nearly naked.

So instead, I settle at the end of the bed and close my eyes. I can't block the sounds of crying, of metal trays being knocked to the floor, or angry screeches as one of the girls is held down for her blood draw. But I can breathe, and I can let the numbness overtake me, pull me away to somewhere else. Anywhere else.

The exam isn't pleasant, but it's at least over quickly. We're told to stay put while our blood tests are run, and so we do. It feels like I'm above the room staring down at someone else in my body as she stares at the cracked linoleum floor. Whatever pattern used to be there is gone, caked in so much grime that it's one big, gray smear with most of the corners chipped off. But it's still better to focus on than what's happening to me. Her. The pathetic inhabitants of this room.

A wheeled machine is rolled out, skipping the first two women. The third is told to lie back, and her abdomen is scanned. No one tells her what they're looking for, or what they find. They simply move on to several other women in the line. There is no rhyme or reason I can see to who they're checking, and my anxiety grows to the weight of an elephant as it gets closer and closer to me. But it's not my exam table they stop at. It's Nell's.

The numbness tries to leave me as alarm takes hold, but I grip it hard as they tell her to lie back, as the tears leak from the corners of her eyes while they scan her. I caress the numbness like a warm blanket as they walk away, leaving her lying there, abandoned.

My eyes are dry as the doctor and nurse confer at the far end of the room. They point at one of the scanned women, then call over one of the cloaked men. He nods, and calls two of his cronies. They grab her by the arms and drag her from the room, not letting her get dressed, or telling us what's going on. Why her? Where were they taking her?

Nell's blue eyes are frightened as she keeps a white-knuckled grip on the exam table beneath her, but the guards don't touch anyone else. Instead the nurse comes out with a tray of gleaming needle-topped syringes, placing it well out of reach. There's one for each of the women they scanned, and she goes down the line injecting each of them.

Nell cries harder when they reach her, but doesn't fight. She clutches her stomach as they walk away, and I can't look at her again. After that, they let us dress, and lead us back through the twisting halls.

16

I hold the numbness tight, walking in front of Nell as we're shoved back into cells. The guards are haphazard, not bothering to check that we're put back into the cells we came from. I'm shoved into a cell close to the gate with a new roommate.

She sighs when she sees me, shaking her head.

"What's your name, honey?"

I don't answer her. I'm not sure that I can, really. So I stand there like a broken doll, a puppet with her strings cut, and stare. She's a tall Black woman with carefully braided hair that brushes the tops of her shoulders. Her features are sharp, and she's underweight for her height. But she's cleaner than anyone else I've seen here, and her clothing isn't torn, like Carla's was. The sheath dress she wears is a vibrant orange, which almost hurts my eyes.

A scuffle outside tugs at my attention, but I ignore it at first. Do I want to see more people being mistreated when I can't do anything about it?

"Demelza!" A man's rough yell breaks through the numbness; like a glass hitting a tile floor, my cocoon shatters and bursts away from me.

I spin and press my face to the scuffed plexiglass, craning my neck to see who's calling my name. And I do. It's Beckett, trying to shove through black-cloaked men. He breaks away, sprinting for the metal gate at the end of the hallway. I'm only one cell away from it, mere feet from him.

"Demelza!" He rattles the gate, as if sheer force of will might propel it open. But it holds fast, and the guard abandons the line of women he was still locking away to run down the hall on this side. He's not needed though. The captors he broke away from are on him in seconds, snatching him back from the gate.

One of them grabs the back of Beckett's neck and rams his face into the metal bars. I pound on the plexiglass, trying to get their attention. He groans loudly on impact but doesn't give up.

"Let me take her with me! Please, whatever my father offered you, I'll double it!"

His father? Has he paid to get him out of here?

"Typical little rich boy," the man seethes at his back. "You think everything's about *money*. But it's *not*." He grinds Beckett's face a little hard into the bars, and I sob.

"She's my match! Please!" He tries again, bargaining even as he keeps his eyes locked with mine.

The man behind him laughs darkly. "Oh, she's your *match*? We'll be sure to give her *extra* special treatment then." He wrenches Beckett off the bars, then slams him into them again, harder this time, and Beckett goes limp. He slides down the bars and the man lets go, letting him fall to the floor with a sickening thud.

They didn't kill him. They *wouldn't*, or else his father wouldn't pay a ransom, right? Surely they wouldn't.

I watch, tears streaming down my cheeks, as they drag his limp body away. The guard inside the cell hallway stops outside my cell and glares at me, all traces of boredom gone now.

His words are muffled as they filter through the thick plexiglass, but the message is crystal clear.

"Troublemakers don't live long here."

I turn my back on the man, walk to the nearest cot, and curl into a ball, my back to my new roommate. She doesn't say a word, simply pulls the blanket up and over me, before turning back to her own cot.

The silence in our cell is deafening as my tears soak the sour bedding wadded under my head.

CHAPTER FIVE

HOLDING

DEMY

The next day I'm woken by someone shaking my shoulders.

"Demelza! Get yourself up. They'll be around to take us out soon, and you need to clean up."

"It's Demy," I groan as I roll onto my back, staring straight at the ugly ceiling. This room has dangling plaster as well, and I wonder how it got damaged. There's nothing in here to throw except the cots, and they've got heavy steel frames.

"Girl, you drop that attitude. You're lucky I'm not calling you *fresh meat* after that display yesterday, and in fact, I might until you prove you've got a brain in that thick skull of yours." She shoves my shoulder again—lightly, like she's not *really* mad—and then goes to straighten her cot's blankets.

"It's not *my fault* the guard came after me. Beckett was one of my matches and was kidnapped with me and my friend." I sit up and my stomach grumbles angrily. It's not the first time I've had stomach cramps from hunger, but they suck just as much as I remember.

"Well, you better get over that quick, or you won't live long enough to be sorry about it." She puts the finishing touch on the corner, tight enough to bounce a quarter off of, and then spins back toward me, her braids flying around her shoulders dramatically.

"What's your name?" I ask.

"Sherese. Nice of you to finally ask." She sniffs, but softens the gesture with a half-cocked grin. "Now, I wasn't kidding—get up and get cleaned up. You're rooming with me, you're going to wash. I don't want to smell you." She points to the sink and toilet, then pointedly turns her back.

I do as she asks, and even though a sink-bath isn't much, I still feel better. More *human*. And for all I've been slipping in and out of shock since I woke up here, I need to hold onto that rational feeling. I can't afford to let myself go numb, give up.

Helplessness is already dragging at me, draining away the fight that I was so desperate to hang onto, and it's been what, a day? I have to do better, or I'll never get out of here. And I need to get us out of here. These men are dangerous, and I refuse to become one of their broken toys.

"So, are they ever going to feed us?" I ask, turning my focus to staying alive.

"Yes. There are always a few hungry days when they go collecting. But then things settle back down once you all fall in line." She gives me a pointed look up and down but doesn't comment on the state of my attire.

Collecting, like we are literally toys for their amusement.

I run my hands down my favorite workout pants nervously, surprised to find my palms are sweating. Being here is existing in a constant state of stress, and my body is showing the signs.

It's amazing how quickly I got into a routine at the NLC, where I had a small degree of safety and normalcy for the first time since childhood. Yet, here I am. Captured from under their noses.

It was all an illusion, and that is a bitter truth.

The door scrapes open, a guard appearing. He's younger than our hallway monitor yesterday. Medium skin tone, blue eyes. Still bald. He eyes Sherese appreciatively before looking at me.

"They saddled you with a new one, beautiful?"

She tosses her long braids over her shoulder and places a hand on her hip. "You know I'm up for the challenge, Zion."

She's on a first name basis with our captors? *Why?*

"You always are. Come on." He grins at her, a hint of lasciviousness to it, but nothing dark. Completely different than yesterday, at our exam.

A shudder rips through me at the memory, and I immediately shut it down. I have to compartmentalize, or else I won't make it.

I could do that, though, and ironically, it was *because* of these men chasing me for half my life that I could. I know how to shut down my feelings and just exist on the razor's edge. I could go back to that place. So I lock down the emotions, the memories of having my privacy violated. Shut away the humiliation, the shame. As I follow Sherese and Zion out the door, there's only one emotion left to simmer on the surface: pure, unadulterated rage.

We're led to a new place, this one at the other end of the hall, away from the common living area we saw yesterday, and all the twisty hallways. This end of the cell block opens up and vomits us into a standard gym-sized room with what must be forty or fifty women already milling about, but there are no hallways or other outlets that I can see at first glance. Picnic-style tables with benches sit in tidy rows in one quarter of the room, but the rest is a rec area with basic prison-yard accouterments; a basketball hoop, some free weights for exercise. My eyes alight on the one thing that never fails to excite me: a rowing machine.

I can't go to it though, without breaking from the line. Nell isn't in my group of women, which worries me. The orderly line breaks apart when we reach the tables. Some of the women go straight to seats, while others go to a small window cut into the cement wall, where trays of food are appearing. The scent of hot food hits me, and while it isn't *terribly* appealing, I'll eat anything at this point that doesn't eat me first.

I head for the window, keeping my eyes peeled for Nell. They are probably moving us in smaller groups, but if I can't find her . . .

I can't bring myself to finish the thought. I have to stay focused, stay calm.

While I wait to reach the window, I scan the room more closely. There are no exterior windows, and no hallways. The only visible break in the unpainted gray block is this food service window, and I can see a sturdy metal roll-down gate that will cover it when not in use. If it's not locked, though, that may be an option for escape.

When it's my turn, a bald man shoves a large, sectioned tray roughly towards me, and I almost don't catch it before it flies to the ground.

"Next," he growls, and I hurry to steady the tray and get out of his sight.

There is a fork and a spoon already at the side of the tray, but no knife is provided. There is rice, what looks like refried beans, and an unidentified meat patty on the side. It smells like some sort of fish, but I couldn't say what. It's gray. The only thing with any real color is half an orange plopped on the side of the tray.

I've had worse.

I scan the tables hopefully, but there's no sign of Nell. So, I wander back to Sherese—her bright orange dress is easy to spot. She waves me into the empty space next to her. Even though she didn't go to the window, there's a tray in front of her. She's got the same rice and beans, but *two* pieces of orange, and what looks like a simple seared chicken breast instead of the mystery meat special.

Is that a benefit of being a long-time resident here, or something more?

I scan the rest of the trays on the table, then my eyes skim over dozens of women. They are all varying degrees of miserable, and sadness builds into a knot behind my breastbone. But I do my best to block that out. Block *them* out.

It's a cold reality; if I let myself get bogged down, I won't be able to think clearly enough to help anyone. If I can get myself and Nell out of here, I can get all the other women out, too. Years on the run have taught me not to get too close, not to let myself feel too deeply while I'm in danger.

Only one other woman has received the same meal as Sherese. She's equally clean and wearing a simple fitted gown, in a vibrant blue. Hers is cut low, showing off her cleavage. I'm seeing the beginnings of a pattern, but don't know what it means yet. There's some small talk floating around the table, surprisingly normal for a table full of women. There are plenty who aren't speaking, though, and I recognize a few of them from our ordeal yesterday. Most of their faces have tear tracks etched through the grime on their cheeks.

"It wouldn't kill them to let us have private showers at least once a week. That's all I'm saying," one of the women grumbles.

"It wouldn't *kill them* to be decent human beings, yet here we are," another snaps.

"Both of you hush, or get off my table," Sherese silences them with a flick of her fingertips.

Lifting my fork, I begin to shovel in my food as the conversation restarts on a different topic. The small talk is minor, nothing much. One of the women tells a story about life before, and her best friend Susan. It's wistful, as if she could just dial her up any time, which makes no sense to me.

When my fork scrapes up the last bit of rice, I ask Sherese, "How long are we here?"

She lifts an eyebrow at my quick eating, when most of the new girls haven't eaten more than a couple bites.

"Maximum of two hours, but if there's trouble, we get cut short. So, don't cause trouble." The look she levels on me brooks no nonsense.

"I wouldn't dream of it," I say, sarcasm edging my tone.

She shakes her head. "Okay, fresh meat. You can use any of the equipment you want, but the showers are considered an open invitation." She levels a pointed look at me.

"Showers?"

She jerks her chin towards the far corner, where three bare showerheads stick out of the wall. There are no curtains, just a few bare cakes of soap laid on the floor. My memories of the watching guards yesterday click into place.

"Who needs a shower?" I mutter, and pick up my tray. There's a bin to drop it in, which I do. And then I start working my way around the room, looking for Nell. I pass a half-hearted pickup game of basketball, give the showers a *wide* berth, and continue around the room.

When I find her, she's huddled in a corner near the free weights, trying to make herself small and unobtrusive.

I sink to my haunches in front of her. The bruise on her face looks worse today, green starting to color the edges as it begins to fade.

When I reach for her hand, she flinches back, and my heart sinks.

"What happened, Nell? You need to eat. It's been a couple days, best I can tell."

She shakes her head and won't make eye contact. Her eyes are red-rimmed, her hair a nest on the back of her head. It's breaking my resolve to see my tiny, spirited friend looking so beaten down.

I try again to capture her hand, and this time she lets me, a squeaking sob breaking free. I pull my orange half from my thigh pocket, break a segment free, and press it into her palm. "Please eat something. We've got to keep your strength up until we can get out of here and get you back to Atlas." The words are a whisper, but they bring tears brimming back to her eyes.

"I can't do this, Demy. It's bringing it all back, and I just— I—"

"Shh, it's okay. You don't have to explain." I urge her hand to her lips, and she finally takes a noncommittal bite of the orange. We've flipped scripts, with her needing extra support, where before she was the one helping me through my anxiety attacks. If she hadn't, I probably wouldn't know what to do for her now. "I know it's awful. But if you can, push that aside. Squeeze it into a little box and

25

screw the lid on tight. Focus on Atlas, on how hard he's going to hug you when you see him again. You know he's looking for us. Beckett is getting out; he can tell them we're still alive. Tell them everything he saw."

Her fingers slide out of my grip and she covers her eyes with the heels of her hands. "I don't want him to see me like this."

"He's not going to care how you look. But I can fix your hair for you if you want."

Nell shakes her head again, so I don't press. Food is more important than a few knots in her hair, so I sit with her quietly and pass her the orange, piece by piece. The silence between us is comforting, in its own way. When the orange is all gone, she finally speaks again.

"You don't have to sit here with me. You like to exercise, right? That's your thing?"

I nod, looking a little wistfully over at the rower. "It is now. After my parents were killed, I was homeless a lot. The gym was a safe place, where I could shower and have a little bit of normalcy." I shrug, feeling awkward sharing the memory.

She surprises me by squeezing my hand. "We all have stuff. It's okay. My uncle was an abusive drunk, and all this—" She blows out a shaking breath, steeling herself to continue. "All of this brings back the nightmares. I thought I was past that, but apparently being imprisoned and smacked around brings it back." Her smile is watery, but I'm still glad to see it, even if it's dark humor. Talking about it is better than pretending, sometimes.

"How's your roommate?" she whispers.

"Interesting. I get the impression she's been here awhile. She knows the guards by name. How about yours?"

"I'm not sure. She just cried all night—not that I can judge." She waves to her own face. "But she wasn't in the medical exam yesterday, so she's been here longer than us, I think."

"Well, hopefully they can give us some clues to how this all works, and if there are any places we might be able to get out. There were a lot of side halls we didn't go down yesterday on the way to the medical exam."

Nell shudders at the unpleasant memory. "I have a bad feeling about that. Why were they running ultrasounds only on some of us? I thought the Cabal killed women, but something feels off."

"Is that what that was?"

"Yeah. Unless something was off in our bloodwork, it seems like they'd have tested us all." A different kind of fear flits across her features before she schools it away.

"Maybe I can ask Sherese. She seems to know what's up around here."

Nell nods, looking out across the room. I'm starting to feel restless. "You should get a tray. You can bring it over here to eat and watch me sweat." I elbow her lightly, but she shakes her head. "You go, I'll watch." Her smile has firmed up into a grimace, now.

"Okay," I agree, crossing to the rower and sticking my feet into the stirrups. The familiar routine helps clear my mind, but I take it easy. I've had no calories for more than twenty-four hours, and I don't know how long it will be until I get another meal.

Eventually an angry buzzer sounds, and women start lining up in front of the guard who brought them in. Nell and I squeeze hands one last time before parting ways.

I shimmy into line behind Sherese and, when the person behind me grumbles, Sherese shoots me a *be careful* look. But she doesn't press the issue, and in a minute the guard opens the gate to take us back to our cells.

Chapter Six

Hunting

Atlas

Fury is my constant companion. It's been a ridiculous *three days* since the attack—time we've used to gather information and manpower, but every minute has been torture. I pace the meeting room, checking my watch for the twentieth time. But people are finally filing in, and I nod to each of them. Easton is first, my ever-punctual second in command. But he still won't meet my eyes; hasn't since Nell was taken.

He feels guilty, even though I was the one with her. I know that much, even though the rest of my memory is patchy. I can't remember how I was downed, or who took her. Only fragments of the scene, of her crying as she was dragged away into the woods. Of a gun, glinting in the afternoon sunlight. No matter how much guilt he's got, it can never match mine.

I should probably take him aside and tell him I'm not angry with him, but I just can't bring myself to say the words until Nell is back at my side, safe and where she belongs. If she can ever forgive me.

Five years. Five years of marriage, and I let her get kidnapped by the bastards in the Cabal. I can barely stand myself. I'm supposed to be the best in the world at private security, and I can't keep my own wife safe? She'll probably divorce me when I get her back, and I deserve it.

Fletcher appears in the doorframe, and I tense. "I don't believe you were invited to this meeting, Mr. Lennox." I keep my tone casual, but the implication is clear. *Get out, and don't make a scene.*

"A fact I'm willing to overlook, given your stress levels right now. Demy is my match, and if there's a plan in place to find her, I deserve to be here." He's calm, collected, and, other than striding further into the room, not budging.

I clench my jaw, the muscle there ticking in aggravation. Easton looks to me for a decision.

"You don't have the clearance for the information that will be shared in this meeting."

"I don't care. I know this is different for you, and maybe it doesn't seem like much. But Demy and I have real feelings for each other, and I was planning to propose to her the day she was taken. In my mind, she's my fiancé. And I am not going to sit idly by and wait for someone else to fix it when my fiancé's life is on the line. And you can either respect that, or I'll do what I swore I never would and call my father to send me a team of lawyers. That is *not* going to speed up the process, and I have no desire to deal with that kind of red tape. I want to help."

I can see in his eyes that it's a threat he's willing to execute, and as annoyed as I am, I have to respect it. Would I have been any different if Nell had been abducted before we'd tied the knot?

Not even remotely. I'd have been standing exactly where he is, and I can't fault him for it.

"You're going to have to sign an NDA and keep your mouth shut." I point off to the side, and he nods in understanding before taking a seat.

The director of this NLC walks in next, and then it's a steady stream. Their head of security walks in, along with a few of their top guards. But then I see four very familiar, worried faces, and I almost break.

Glitch is in the door first, his usual collection of tech in a messenger bag slung over his shoulder. He's aged some since the last time we were at a New Life Center, with a bit of salt starting to show at his temples, but then so have I. He comes straight for me and offers a hand. I use it to pull him into a hug. The smaller man returns it, slapping my back. "We just landed. I've been digging since you sent word, and I've got some things to share."

I nod, but don't have time to dig into it yet, because Sadie and Patrick are right behind him, her arms already flung wide. She's got a heavily pregnant belly leading the way when she practically strangles me with her hug.

"We're going to get them back, Atlas. We *have to*." I can hear the tears in her voice, and I squeeze her a little bit tighter. She and Nell have been best friends ever since the beginning, and my wife would hate how torn up Sadie is right now. But if the roles were reversed, Nell would be just the same. Their bond runs deep and it runs true.

Patrick doesn't go in for the hug, opting for a firm handshake instead. It's served with a side of Kingly decorum, which I've come to expect. He always keeps things professional when we're in public, but when it's just our group he lets his hair down, and it's the same old Patrick. It's odd to see both sides of a public figure.

But over the years, I've gotten used to it. He's got his job, and I've got mine.

He's *never failed quite as epically as I have.* The thought nearly pulls me into a spiral, but my years of crisis training keep me on task. I refuse to break down when my wife is out there, afraid and waiting on me to rescue her.

Mav, our pilot and my dear friend, stands behind him, her expression grave. She doesn't hug me because she doesn't hug. But she gives me a firm nod. "We're going to decimate whoever took 'er. Scorched earth, you hea' me?" Her Cajun accent is stronger when she's angry, and I've only seen her this livid twice in my life. She looks ready to set something on fire.

She'll have to get in line.

They take seats, as the last few people file in. Peter slips in next to Sadie, giving her a quick hug before focusing on me and Easton, where we stand at the front of the room. I've asked him to lead the meeting, so that I can focus on the details.

"Thank you all for being here. We've got our work cut out for us. Roger, any update on the missing guards?"

He shakes his head. "Negative. Two are still missing, presumed injured or dead."

"Okay. We'll keep looking; it's not their MO to take men, but—"

"Actually, I have some information on that," Glitch butts in, pushing his glasses up his nose.

"All right, what've you got?" Easton asks.

"I was able to recover some of the missing footage from the rear of the compound. Carter, one of the missing guards, was knocked out and dragged into the woods. If he hasn't been found yet, we need to search the southwest quadrant in the forest for him; he's likely in need of medical attention. Or . . ." His face looks sad, and he shakes his head. "Well, let's get the medical staff out there ASAP. Lars, however, is a bit different." Glitch presses his lips into a line I don't like, and then taps a few times on his tablet.

It feels like I should remember *something* about Lars, but I can't pinpoint it for the life of me. Was he there when Nell was taken? Pain throbs behind my eyes, and I resist the urge to dig the heel of my palms into them, do something to counterbalance the ache.

The large wall screen flickers for a second, and then we're watching a surveillance feed. It shows Carter and Lars, standing at the back of the gymnasium, which is the building closest to the lake, where Nell, Demy, and Beckett were taken.

We all watch in silence as Lars slips a rock from his pocket, fingers it for a second, and then when Carter scans away from him, tosses it toward the corner of the building, so it bounces off and makes a racket. He jogs behind Carter to "check it out," and then as soon as they round the corner, a scuffle is heard.

Glitch taps the tablet again, and the angle changes; one of the cameras from the side of the building shows a passed-out Carter, with Lars dragging him under the arms in the direction of the heavily wooded southwest corner of the property. Well, that answers the question of whether he was involved. But I still can't remember if he was involved with Nell's actual kidnapping, or just clearing the way for something else.

He taps one more time, and the image freezes, zooming in on Lars's face, which is a mask of determination as he drags Carter's limp body. "I think it's obvious that Lars was a mole, working for the Cabal."

I swear, turning on the leader of the NLC's guard. "I want every scrap of information you've got on him. I don't care how insignificant; we need to figure out how they slipped him past us."

"Yes, sir."

"Have you got anything else, Glitch?"

"Two more things. My research into Demy's"—he glances at the extended audience in the room, then meets my eyes pointedly—"*unique background* led me to some interesting things. It seems her heritage is actually European, which is something we didn't know previously."

"I don't see how that helps us locate her now," the director says drily.

"I suppose not." Glitch gives her a genial smile, glossing over the information only we know. I glance over at Fletcher, to see if he has any idea what we're talking about, but his face shows no signs of significance at the information, only surprise.

But it's pertinent to us, since she's the result of a genetically modified embryo, which was thought destroyed. If the Cabal has been tracking her since birth, and the embryo is European, does that mean someone from across the ocean has their fingers in the Cabal, too? Our intelligence has never given any hints that the terrorist organization existed anywhere except the NAA. I'll ask him to dig deeper when we've got some privacy.

"And the second thing?" Easton prods.

"Oh, ah—I've found a potential drop site for the SUVs that took the girls. A farmer reported some suspicious abandoned vehicles to the local police, and it just pinged my tracking program that they're located about . . . four hours from here, by car."

I snap at the director, "Get me a chopper, now."

She purses her lips in annoyance at the command, but nods to one of her employees, who races from the room.

"I'm coming." Peter stands, crossing his arms over his chest.

I nod, not worried about anyone else who wants to come.

"Me too," Fletcher is on his feet in an instant, a thunderous expression replacing his usually genial smile.

"You're not coming," I argue. "We have no idea what we'll find, or where we'll go next. You and your family history are a liability I'm not willing to add to the mix."

He places two hands on the u-shaped conference table, and leans over it. "Unless you are willing to physically restrain me, I'm getting on that chopper."

"Whoa. Let's all take a deep breath," Patrick says, standing and placing himself in between the two of us. "There's room for everyone who wants to come, and I'll personally accept responsibility for Fletcher's presence."

The two of them meet eyes for a second, and Fletcher relaxes, nodding his thanks.

"I'll fly," Mav states, *not* a question. The director shoves her chair back and leaves the room, but I couldn't care less about her pride, or her opinions. She can have opinions again once my wife and the others are home.

"Let's move!" I'm already halfway to the door, and whoever's coming better do it quick, because I'm not waiting another second.

CHAPTER SEVEN

FAVORS

DEMY

As soon as we're locked back in our cell, I start peppering Sherese with questions.

"So, how often are we taken out to the food-and-exercise area?"

"Twice per day, but they always skip a few days whenever a new batch of girls is brought in." She sinks down onto her cot, and slides off her shoes.

"And how often is that?"

She waves her hand around our bare walls. "Do you see a calendar in here? I don't know. Every once in a while."

"So not like every week?"

"No. Every few months, if I had to guess."

"Gotcha." I sit on my own cot, and wait for her to get comfortable with her back propped up against the wall. She has an actual, honest-to-God pillow, and she sticks it behind her for cushion. But when she starts to shut her eyes, I interrupt. "So, what about the whole medical thing? They gave some of the girls ultrasounds yesterday, but not all of us. My friend Nell got one."

She closes her eyes anyways, but still answers. "If you were smart, you'd stop calling her that."

"Calling her what?" I ask, confused.

"Your *friend*. Friends are dangerous. You've got roommates, and guards. That's it."

"Okay. But what's with the ultrasounds, do you know?"

"What am I, the Oracle of Delphi? No, I am not. You're not allowed in here if you're pregnant. They check your hormones, and if they think it's necessary they scan you. Now shut your mouth so I can get some beauty rest."

It's my turn to sigh as she crosses her hands over her stomach and pretends I'm not here.

But at least I got some useful information first. Pregnancy is against the rules, which makes sense. I don't know much about the Cabal's purpose, beyond being the boogeyman women everywhere are afraid of.

I always thought they just killed whoever they took, but that's clearly not the case.

Our next trip to the holding area comes that evening, as promised. This time Nell is in line for a food tray, and the sight calms my nerves. We just have to stay alive long enough to either get ourselves out, or have Atlas find us. The way that man looks at Nell, there's no way he's not going to burn the world down to find her.

And what about you, Demy? Who's burning the world down to get you back?

Two faces swim before my vision, wrapped up in a tangle of confusing emotions. I'd been so sure it was Fletcher, and yet . . . that kiss with Beckett had surprised me.

Granted, one kiss didn't mean we were compatible for life, but he wasn't going down without a fight. And I couldn't stop seeing his fight to reach me, and then him crumpling to the floor and being dragged away.

Fletcher feels like a distant dream, his memories wrapped up in soft cotton, isolated from this hell-hole.

Maybe it's best that they stay that way.

I shake off the pointless questions and step into line for my next meal. But this time, I watch Sherese, and the woman in blue. Sure enough, they both go straight to sit at the tables, not bothering to join the line. A few minutes later—while I'm still waiting for a tray—two of the Cabal men come out of the hallway, trays in hand. Each of them stops next to a woman and slides the tray onto the table in front of her. Sherese's man lays a gentle stroke on her cheek, whispering something into her ear before turning to leave. The other man, however, grips her chin and lays a devouring kiss directly on her lips. I turn away when her arms curl around his neck, not interested in watching them.

My stomach turns, but it makes a twisted sort of sense. They're both cleaner, wearing nice clothing, and receiving special food.

And pillows, I remember, thinking back to the small comforts Sherese has in our cell. She's always taken to the same cell, and it's also stocked with soap, toothpaste, and toothbrushes—one of which she lent me.

I finally get my tray, and then see Nell hovering off to the side, waiting for me. I nod towards Sherese, and the two of us squeeze onto the bench at her table.

The men have both gone, thankfully, so there are no more awkward displays.

Our food is much the same as this morning, but instead of a mystery fish cake, it's a cold chicken salad. It's a little bit gritty, but I shovel down every unpleasant bite. Nell's picking at her food, but I shoot her a pointed look.

Keep up your strength, girl. Don't let them win.

She puts a few more bites in her mouth, at least. I'll take it. She can't shut down, no matter how bad it gets, if we're going to get out of here.

A fight breaks out before everyone's trays are even clear—one of the new girls who received an ultrasound, and a redhead who I don't recognize—they're pulling each other's hair and screaming, and in an instant our prison guards descend upon them. They're wrenched apart unceremoniously, and Sherese sighs a few spots down. She takes one last bite of her fruit, then stands and walks to the gate.

I grab Nell's hand and follow her. The blue-dress woman is right behind us, and she looks us up and down as she steps into line behind us.

"Got a new pet already, Sherese? That didn't work out so well for you last time." She flips silky blonde hair over one shoulder and levels a scathing look at Sherese.

"Why don't you mind your own business, Emma? And quit letting that man paw you at the dinner table. The sight puts me off my food." Sherese doesn't turn as she delivers the cut down, and Emma huffs behind me.

"Better to keep him happy than skate on the edge, like *you*. Unless you *like* the punishment." Emma's voice is a pointed dagger, and I see Sherese's shoulders tense since I'm standing a few inches from them. But she ignores the barb, instead knocking on the gate with the flat of her hand.

"Manuel!" she calls down the hall, and waves, and her man jogs toward us. He's not bad looking, if you didn't find his cult life utterly repulsive, which I do. Pale-olive skin and warm brown eyes are the only things that distinguish him from every man down here.

"Another fight?" He tsks and pulls a key out of his cloak. He fits it quickly into the gate and waves the four of us through. The other women are all either frozen in place or jeering at the fighters.

"Come on, let's get you out of there." He waves us through, then quickly shuts and re-locks the gate behind us, before shuffling us down to our cells. Emma he puts in alone, and when he reaches Sherese's cell, he looks at both me and Nell after she walks in. "Who's in with Sherese?"

"Come on, fresh meat. I'm not training up another one."

I sigh at the ridiculous nickname, and give Nell a quick nod goodbye before going in.

"Although, you showed some sense today. Maybe you've got a chance."

I let her compliment hang in the air for a few beats before asking more cautiously, "So, you and Manuel . . ." I leave it to dangle, hoping she'll fill in the blanks. I need information more than I need to offend her.

"He's my boyfriend." She stares me down, as if challenging me to say otherwise.

"Right, but how does that work, exactly?" I sit on the edge of my cot, trying to keep any judgment out of my voice. I don't look down on her for the choice; she's got her way of staying alive, and I've got mine. Something clicked in my mind when Manuel unlocked that gate for us.

She cocks one eyebrow, considering me. Whatever she sees on my face must pass the test, because she leans forward on her elbows. "Look, it's not for everyone, okay? It's hard to overlook, well, everything. But if I'm going to be down here, why would I choose to be miserable? Not all of these men are creeps. Manuel is very sweet, and he doesn't ask a lot. In return, my time here is a lot less awful. I don't have to go to the exams, and he brings me gifts when he can."

She pulls a small notebook and pen from under her pillow, running her thumb lovingly over the cover.

"Are you a writer?"

She nods, but tucks them carefully back away instead of answering.

"And Emma?"

Her upper lip curls into a sneer. "She's the worst kind of woman. Thinks having a man down here makes her a big deal. And she likes to toy with people. Just stay away from her."

I nod, having no problem with that. Girl drama isn't my cup of tea. I prefer genuine people, or no people at all. Luckily, since we're stuck together, Sherese falls into the former category.

She seems done with the conversation, though, and starts washing up for the evening, slipping quietly into a sleep set instead of her vibrant dress. When she's done, I also brush my teeth and drink some water from the sink. My mind is buzzing.

A boyfriend with a key might be *exactly* what I need to get out of here. I've got some small hand-to-hand skills, and if he was distracted, I might be able to incapacitate a single man, steal a key, and make a break for it. But if I fail, or end up with a guard who's not so *sweet* . . .

I can't think about that.

There are some lines I won't cross, and when our cell door scrapes quietly open sometime late in the night, and Sherese gets up to leave with Manuel, I know that's one of them.

CHAPTER EIGHT

ENDS AND BEGINNINGS

FLETCHER

The chopper drops through the air, and if I hadn't been told that Mav was an expert pilot, with tens of thousands of hours in the chair, I'd be very certain we were all going to crash and die. I grip the straps of my harness and grit my teeth through it, though. Nobody else is panicking, and I'm not about to be the wuss who freaks out.

Mav threads the chopper through a very small opening in the dense cluster of towering pines, dropping us straight to flat earth, and if I wouldn't be mocked, I'd probably kiss the grass under my feet when we step out of the chopper.

When she sets us down, her wry voice crackles through the helmet speakers. "You're up, boys. I don't do nature outside the cockpit. But I'll be ready to fly whenever you're back."

My stomach isn't going to settle for a week after this.

But I know whatever Demy is going through right now is worse. And that thought steels my spine, and pushes me through it. In any other circumstance, I'd love a new adventure. But right now, it's the last thing on my mind. I won't lie, though—the spongy grass under my feet is welcome, as we cluster outside the door and wait for instructions.

"Okay, I've gotten the report from the owner. The SUVs were dropped about a mile and a half northeast of our current location. He runs pigs and goats in the area, and apparently one of them came back chewing a piece of trash. He investigated, and found the abandoned vehicles," Peter says, reading the details off of a miniature tablet.

Apparently the guy is high up in the NAA police, but *also* one of Queen Sadie's brothers, which is why he's really here. I don't care what motivates him, only that he's helping me get my girl back in one piece.

Please, let her be in one piece.

We hike through the woods in near silence, each of us scanning the forest for clues. I don't see anything significant, just animal tracks and piles of pine needles. Easton spots the vehicles first.

"Over there!" He points us toward them.

The SUVs are tucked into a deep thicket, and we spread out to assess the area. It's a little bit scary how well thought out this hiding spot is. If a herd of hungry goats hadn't eaten through their carefully chosen cover, it probably would never have been found. People typically stay well away from thick, thorny brambles.

But on closer inspection, there are sawn-off limbs and a hidden piece of chain link underneath some of the foliage, which they would have pulled out of the way to drive the vehicles in.

"How far do we think they got with three unconscious bodies? I don't see any tracks going in another direction, though I suppose if it were a lighter vehicle, the vegetation could have already sprung back, now that it's been a few days," Peter muses aloud.

"Not far on foot without being seen, and because of the time of day they were snatched, it would have still been daylight when they ended up here. Are we sure the farmer's not in on it?"

Peter shrugs. "I didn't interview him, but the locals say he's a good citizen in the community."

"Let's talk to him ourselves. I don't see anything here to indicate where they went or how they traveled."

I stare forlornly around, running my finger over the damaged pine, the rough-cut wood oozing sap. Even with all my time in the woods, I don't see anything here that's useful. The trucks themselves are clean, and without a fingerprinting kit, we have no way of tracing who drove them. I'm sure Peter will call that in as part of the follow up, but for now . . . we're back to square one.

By the time night falls, Peter has spoken with the farmer and agreed he's not involved. A larger team of searchers arrived by car and helped us canvas ten square miles of forest, and we found nothing. Not a set of tracks, not a scrap of cloth.

We have no more leads and we're no closer to finding Demy. We start the moonlit hike back to the helicopter in tense silence, and I can't help but feel that every day we don't find her is a day closer to not ever finding her. And I just can't live with that.

Peter slaps me on the back as we climb into the helicopter, face grim but determined. "The Cabal is good at covering their tracks, but eventually they're going to slip up. And when they do, we'll be ready."

Chapter Nine

CAT FIGHT

Demy

The next morning, I'm once again woken by Sherese shaking my shoulder. She doesn't give me any guff, though, just wakes me and points to the sink. I don't argue; if she's willing to share her hygiene supplies, I'm grateful.

"Thanks for the toothbrush," I say after rinsing my mouth out.

"Welcome." She seems broodier than usual, and I can't help but wonder if her night went badly. She's already dressed in vibrant orange, no traces of her nighttime outing anywhere.

She stays quiet as we make our way to the holding area again, this time for breakfast. The days have a simple routine, but also a boring one. There is nothing to keep us busy in our cells, and yesterday we were out of them for less than three hours, because of the fight. I'm practically climbing the walls.

This morning I'm going to keep observing, but after breakfast and a good, hard row on the machine. I have to keep myself physically ready to escape, too. And now that the drugs are fully out of my system, I'm antsy to make a move. *Any* move. But moving *too* soon or without enough information will get me killed.

It's a battle of two different instincts, and it's exhausting. But as I'm handed my usual tray of rice, beans, and fish cakes, there's nothing to do for it.

Nell sits next to me with a disgusted look on her face, prodding her mystery fish with her fork. "What is this?"

"Seafood," I mumble around a mouthful. My childhood scrounging turned up worse food than this, but clearly hers didn't.

She wrinkles her nose and eats the rice, at least.

"Beans too, princess, or you'll lose muscle." I point my fork at her until she swats it away, shaking her head at my stupid teasing.

"It's cute that you think I have any muscles to lose. I've been in med school for years; I've got great triceps from carrying medical textbooks, and that's it." She shovels a bite of beans in anyways, and I smile in triumph.

"Well, we can't lose those, now, can we?" Sherese cuts in, amusement coloring her voice.

"Exactly," I agree, still shoveling down my food.

"How'd you manage to get into med school?" Sherese asks, suddenly interested in my far-too-quiet friend.

I'm done in minutes while they discuss Nell's special school waiver, and after a quick word to Nell, I'm on a rower, sinking blissfully into the familiar motion.

Some people meditate, some people pray. I lose myself in hard physical activity. And lose myself, I do. Until I stop with a yelp when my elbow cracks painfully against something solid.

"Are you kidding me? You just ran right into me!" an outraged feminine voice shrieks from right behind me.

"What? Why would you walk directly into the track?" I loosen the stirrups, and slip my feet out of them. Before I can stand and turn, though, the woman grabs a handful of my hair and *yanks*.

White-hot pain lights up my scalp, and I fling an *intentional* elbow back toward her ribs to break her grip. My attacker screeches in rage.

"You're going to regret that, you little priss!"

I'm on my feet and in a fighting stance before she can make good on the threat.

It's the same redhead who got into it yesterday and cut our afternoon outing short. *And here she is, trying to start something again.*

"I don't want to fight with you, lady—I'm just trying to use the machine. We can drop this right now," I say, but don't drop my defensive stance.

Burn me once, shame on you. Burn me twice? *Never going to happen.*

"It's Erin," she snaps as she lunges for me, hands curled into angry claws. I half leap to the side, but it's hard to completely dodge around the workout equipment. One of my heels clips a kettlebell, and her nails catch and rake down my forearm, leaving angry red trails through my skin.

I swear like a sailor and swing, landing a solid punch to her shoulder. It knocks her back a step, but she screeches like a banshee the whole time, drawing *far* too much attention. Guards are swarming toward us, and Nell is running from the picnic tables, trying to back me up. But Erin is already flying at me again. This time she's aiming those damnable claws at my face.

I throw up a forearm to block her wild attack, and use a leg sweep that Peter taught me to take her legs out from under her.

She lands flat on her back with a grunt of pain, the screams cutting off as all her breath is knocked out of her. I take several big steps back, trying to distance myself from the pointless attack.

I hold my hands up as the guards swarm us, shaking my head to ward Nell off. There's no point in her getting wrapped up in this stupid mess, too.

Her face is stricken as two guards wrestle my bleeding arms behind my back and start dragging me from the area. I'm satisfied to say it takes three guards to get Erin up on her feet. Her face is red with humiliation when they drag her towards the gate behind me, and somehow, even though I don't know what precipitated the attack, I know it's not over.

To my surprise, I'm taken through the twisting halls toward the medical exam room again. I have better luck counting the hallways this time, and even see a few people walking in and out of doors in the side hall. The few glimpses I catch look like bedrooms, though, and not escape options. It's okay though. If I had to be attacked out of the blue, at least I'm getting some information out of it.

When they shove me through the door into the exam room, the nurse startles at the abrupt intrusion.

"What's happened now?" she asks, irritation quickly replacing her surprise. She has a sandwich in her hand as she points to the nearest exam table.

"Another fight," one of the guards answers her. I take a closer look at him and realize it's not our usual hallway guard. It's Manuel, Sherese's "boyfriend."

"Is this the troublemaker?"

"Not this time. The redhead apparently wants a week in solitary—attacked her out of the blue and scratched her arms all up."

"It's never out of the blue, Manuel." She gives the man a scathing look, as if she knows he's *involved* with one of the women, and doesn't approve. More than one, maybe? "I'll call Franz and see what he wants us to do with her. She's well past three strikes."

I eye Manuel skeptically when he releases my wrists and nods for me to get on the table. It's ridiculous of me to be protective of Sherese, but she's been good to me in her own way, and I don't want to see her hurt any worse.

Though maybe she wouldn't care if he was also with one of the other girls. She's hard to read.

More importantly, what happens after three strikes? And who is Franz? Someone in charge of the Cabal? I suppose it's logical that *someone* is in charge, though in my mind they've always been this nebulous hydra of an organization; a many-headed monster that comes back after you no matter how many heads you cut off or run away from.

The door to the infirmary slams open, Erin still screeching as the three guards drag her in. She's kicking and causing a ruckus, which elicits another sigh from the nurse.

"Don't move, don't cause trouble in here or I'll knock you out next. Capiche?" The nurse warns me sternly before turning to assess Erin.

I nod, keeping silent and stone-still as she turns her back on me to go subdue the other woman. Erin screams and thrashes in the entryway, one of the guards swearing as she bites him on the hand. The nurse jogs across the room to a locked cupboard, flips the numbers on the lock until it clicks open, and pulls out a pre-loaded syringe.

"Hold her!" she snaps as she comes closer.

The guard who she bit backhands Erin across the face, the sound loud in the suddenly still room. She goes silent under the assault, red blooming on her cheek as she slowly shakes her head, clearly dizzy from the impact.

The sight makes me sick to my stomach, but the nurse doesn't miss the opportunity, jabbing the needle into the crook of her arm.

Erin hisses in pain but doesn't jerk away as the needle is withdrawn.

"It might take five minutes, so don't go anywhere yet. But get her on the bed, so she doesn't hit her head when it kicks in."

The guards nod and lead the already-drooping Erin to the opposite end of the infirmary. The nurse watches with her hands on her hips, and a disappointed look on her face.

Once Erin's out, she fastens her to the exam table with padded leather straps. I watch it all with mute horror. Erin shouldn't have attacked me, but the sight of the straps tightening over her limp form sends bile climbing up the back of my throat.

They could do that to any one of us, and I don't think they'd need a fight to justify it. Once Erin is restrained, all but Manuel and one other guard disperse, and the nurse comes back over toward me as I silently watch her every move.

She examines my arms carefully, shaking her head the entire time. "They're surface level, but fingernails can harbor some nasty bacteria. I'm going to have to clean these with an anti-bacterial and then put ointment and a wrap on both arms. Do you exercise?" She finally looks up, meeting my eyes.

"I was on a rower when she attacked me."

"Ah. You shouldn't receive a strike for this given Erin's history"—she pauses and looks at Manuel, who nods in confirmation—"but you will need to limit physical activity or anything that

51

causes you to sweat for two days, and then come back for the bandages to be removed."

"Okay," I grumble.

She snorts in amusement at my dour tone, and then dons some fresh gloves.

The anti-bacterial wipes suck, but the ointment she swipes painstakingly over each scratch is soothing. By the time she's finished gauzing and wrapping a self-adhesive bandage to cover it all from my wrists to my elbows, the ointment has completely numbed the burn from my wounds.

"Thanks," I tell her as she strips off the gloves and starts to clean up. She looks up in surprise, clearly not used to being thanked for her work here.

"You're welcome . . .?"

"Demy."

"Nice to meet you, Demy. I'm Annie."

I nod. Then Manuel takes me by the wrist, ready to get back to his regular duties, whatever those may be. Or just to check on Sherese. Either way, he bustles me down the hall, and I have to walk fast to keep up with him.

CHAPTER TEN

BECKETT

FLETCHER

I only intended to feel closer to Demy tonight when I climbed this big oak tree outside the men's dormitory. It's silly, really. We only climbed it once, but that night under the stars is imprinted on my memory. And now that she's gone, I find myself willing to be silly if it means I get another hit of that feeling.

I miss her. I miss the way she made me think, the way she smiled at me—it was the only *shy* thing about her, which felt important. I miss talking to her.

The dorms are empty now, sitting dark in the night, so there's no one to disturb as I shimmy up the tree.

I lean into the feeling of bark biting my fingertips, the smell of sap and the crisp night air comforting me as I make my way up to the second-story branch, and then light-foot along the limb. My shoe skids a bit as I land on the roof, but I manage to settle down in the same space without causing myself bodily harm. It's a cloudy night, nothing like the star-filled dream night I spent here with Demy. But it fits my mood. My back has barely kissed the shingles when a low voice has me jolting back upright.

"What in the wide green world are you doing up there?" I peer carefully down over the edge, and see Glitch staring back up at me, mouth hanging open.

"Thinking," I say. Which is true. I don't think he needs to know that I'm pining after a woman. Though of all the men I've met, he seems the least likely to judge.

He pushes his glasses up his nose before responding. "The only thing I'd be thinking about is falling to my death. You're not going to jump, are you?"

"Not unless I want a sprained ankle, no."

"Ahh." He doesn't say anything else, but he also doesn't leave. The silence gets awkward pretty quickly, and I start to lie back down—I suppose he'll wander off eventually—but he calls out. "Wait!"

So I lean back over the edge, waiting. "Yes?"

"Would you mind coming down? I'd like to discuss something with you."

I choke down a sigh. "Sure. Give me a minute."

With one last regretful look up at the overcast sky, I shimmy back down the tree, until I can safely drop to the ground. I land with a solid thud, and Glitch winces.

"What's up?" I ask, dusting my hands off on my jeans.

"Let's sit." He points to the porch, where a two-seater wooden swing waits.

"O-kay." I follow him up onto the porch, and reluctantly take a seat on the swing. It's not made for two full-grown men, and our shoulders bump together awkwardly as he starts us swinging.

"I won't keep you long, I just wanted to see where you were at on a few things," he says, picking at his sleeve hesitantly.

"Like what?" I ask, curiosity piqued.

"Well, had Demy shared much with you about her past?" He's giving me a really intense look, as if there's a very specific thing he wants to know.

"I know she was homeless after her parents died and moved around a lot before coming here. She had a hard life."

"That's good—that's a really good start."

"A start on what?"

"Well," he says, raking a hand through his hair, knocking one arm of his glasses askew, and fixing it in the same motion. "Demy's not your average girl."

I barely restrain a snort at that. I knew that from the moment I met her. She's observant, and cautious, but also fiercely strong and smart. I've never met anyone like her, and I'm deeply afraid I never will again. But I keep all of that to myself, waiting.

"Demy's parents adopted her. But it wasn't your typical adoption. She's from a batch of genetically modified embryos that we previously thought were destroyed. I've recently traced them back to Europe, but we still don't know the full truth of her differences, or how they may impact her. We may never know, except through observation. Much of the science around gene modification was banned, and research destroyed to prevent further steps forward in the wake of the Sterilization Vector."

Something cracks under my palm, and a sharp pain has me looking down. I've gripped the arm of the swing so hard, it's cracked off and sent a sliver of wood into my palm. Crap.

"You okay, over there? Still breathing?"

I nod, not quite capable of words yet as I pinch the splinter and snatch it out. How the heck do you modify a human?

"Is she—is she okay? I mean she's not going to spontaneously die or anything, right? Or turn into one of those creepy robot clones from the old movies?" It's an asinine question, but it's all I've got. My brain has taken a dive off the sci-fi deep end.

Glitch laughs, a short sharp burst at my questions. "No, nothing like that. Best as I can tell—and I'm no geneticist, but I can get by with research as well as the next guy—the only modifications made were to her reproductive genes."

Reproductive genes.

I'm scared to ask.

I *have* to ask.

"Does that mean she can't have kids?" The words tumble out in slow-motion, and I instantly want to suck them back in. But Glitch doesn't judge me.

"Uh, no, we don't think that's what it means. More likely the opposite, actually, given her high match rates with you and both of the other men. But given why you're in this program, combined with the current situation . . . we felt it was time you knew the whole story. Or, at least as much of it as we've got. There's a clause in the paperwork everyone signs that your final three matches are entitled to know of any major medical impacts, so it's on the up and up for you to know. And I hope it doesn't change your opinion of her, but after yesterday, when you insisted on going on the raid, we all agreed you should know. We didn't want to share it in the broader meeting, but you two could be trying to have kids one day, which makes it relevant. So . . ."

"Yeah, so," I murmur halfheartedly. My brain is spinning out, like a car on black ice.

"Well, I'll let you get back to your thinking," Glitch says, slapping his knees before moving to stand.

I reach out on reflex, stopping him from jumping up. "Would you stay for a while? I could use a friend. This is all . . . a lot."

"Of course, man. As long as I get to stay off the roof."

I chuckle at that, and the levity is a welcome relief.

We swing in silence a few minutes, and I ignore the feeling that we're like two teenage girls, gossiping on a swing. Maybe they've got crap to sort out, too.

My wrist comm dings, but I ignore it.

She's not going to die, or be physically harmed by the mods. The only changes are to her reproduction. Glitch said he hopes it doesn't change my opinion of her, but I get the feeling that's code for, *don't walk out on her.*

Would anybody really do that? Just leave, when she's been kidnapped? We haven't known each other long, granted, but the feelings are real. And the longer I sit and think about it, the more resolved I become.

I'm not leaving. Not while she's gone, not once we get her back. There are assistive technologies now, so even if she has trouble having kids, we could work it out, so long as she's open to the idea. And if she's not, or it just won't work, we can apply to adopt, right?

Whatever the future holds for us, I'd like to give it a shot with her.

"Do you have any idea why someone would want to modify her reproductive genes?" I ask, circling back around to the original topic.

"Oh, now that's interesting. My best guess, based on which genes they modified, is that they were trying to improve her fertility. Genes impact a lot. Women are born with their entire lifetime supply of eggs, so they could have been trying to increase that number, though I don't know if that's actually possible at the embryonic stage. But I suspect that they were either trying to prolong her childbearing years, or increase the odds of multiples. It's not possible to say for sure without finding their actual research, but that's my hypothesis."

"So you're saying that if they succeeded, we might actually end up with, like . . . twins?"

"Twins, triplets, quads . . . or her still being able to conceive well into her late fifties. There's no way to know"

My feet drop to the porch, thudding loudly and stopping the swing mid-arc. "Wow."

He slaps me on the back, then gives my shoulder a jovial shake. "Hey, you're here to have kids, right?"

"Yeah," I splutter, overwhelmed by the idea of more than one kid at once. It's not a common thing these days. I don't know any twins, actually, let alone triplets or *more*. I'm just not going to think about that. We've swung between two wildly different ends of the spectrum.

My wrist comm dings again, and Glitch nudges my arm. "You gonna answer that?"

I lift my arm, not even checking who it is, just grateful for anything to think about that's not trying to keep four children alive simultaneously. Four *infants*. We're going to need nannies. Like, a lot of them.

I guess it's a good thing I'm loaded. I drag an exhausted hand over my face, trying to wipe away the shock.

"Yeah," I say, still staring at the dark boards under our feet in my state of shock.

"Fletcher? It's Beckett."

My head snaps up, mine and Glitch's gazes crashing together like a train wreck.

"Where are you?"

"I'm not sure. They dumped me in the middle of nowhere."

"Don't move, don't blink, don't disconnect the line. I can track your location. I already pinged Atlas, he's on the way," Glitch's words are the only thing faster than his fingertips as they move over the tablet. But I don't care about that. Only one person matters.

"Are the women with you? Demy, Nell?" I hold my breath, my stomach twisting itself into sick knots as I anticipate all of the awful things he could be about to say.

Triangles pop up on the screen, and Glitch pauses, watching intently.

It feels like I'm about to explode with anticipation.

Beckett's voice crackles, as if the connection isn't solid. "No, they're not here. But before they took me out of their bunker, Demy was still alive."

"I've got it! New Texas, pretty far south." Glitch pumps a fist into the air.

Atlas sprints up the porch steps, a look of fearsome determination on his face as all the blood drains from mine at what Beckett *hasn't* said.

"Are the women with him?" He barks the question, eyes narrowing on my comm. His hands clench and unclench into fists at his side, and I get the impression he wants to rip it off me, force the answers out of Beckett even half a second sooner.

"No, he was just telling us about them," I say, the words coming out half choked.

"Nell? Is she okay?" Atlas demands.

"I didn't see Nell. Demy was locked inside a cell with a different woman."

Atlas doesn't say anything. Doesn't move, doesn't breathe for a full heartbeat. Then he's an explosion of fury. He cocks back a fist and punches one of the wooden support beams that holds up the porch roof. Wood cracks under the assault as he continues beating it, until he gets tired of punching, then grips the railing on either side and unleashes a volley of kicks.

His steel-toed combat boots have more impact, and in a matter of minutes, the bottom of the beam gives way with a mighty crack, and I duck as the roof over us creaks ominously.

"Atlas!" Glitch scolds him, completely nonplussed by the display of vicious rage. "We don't have enough information yet for that kind of attitude."

"Not now, Glitch." Atlas's head hangs, and he drops both palms to the sagging rail beside the beam he just broke.

"I've got a location. We can get there in a few hours, pick him up, and see if anything he knows can help us find the girls. If Demy is still alive, there's a very good chance that Nell is, too."

Atlas nods but doesn't otherwise move.

"They wouldn't let them stay together. They've probably separated them on purpose," I add, trying to give the man some hope to cling to.

I'd want it, in his shoes.

"How long has it been since you saw her?" I direct the question to my comm.

"I'm not sure. My head's fuzzy, like they drugged me again. I'd guess at least a day?" There's a pause, and then he says, "I see a chopper. Is that you guys already?"

I hear the sound of blades cutting the air in the background and shoot a skeptical look at Glitch.

"No, that's not us. Beckett, can you see any markings on the aircraft?"

No response.

"Beckett?"

CHAPTER ELEVEN

THE THICK OF IT

DEMY

Manuel puts me back in the cell with Sherese, gives her a curt nod, and then locks us in without a look back.

"Okay, look, I know your whole thing is to lay low, but I swear—" I turn towards her, already trying to ease the tempest I can feel building.

"No, fresh meat, this time it wasn't your fault. It was mine."

My jaw drops, mouth hanging open like a fish. I snap it shut, processing. "How? You didn't tell her to attack me, right . . .?"

"No, of course not. I would never. But, she had her eye on Manuel. Manuel picked me. She's had it out for me ever since, but couldn't strike *me* without repercussions. You, however . . . aren't protected. I guess she figured you were the next best thing, since I've taken you under my wing."

I groan and drop down onto my thin cot mattress, not caring that the steel frame digs into the backs of my thighs. The numbing agent in the cream is wearing off, and my arms are starting to throb again. I would kill for a hot shower and a couple ibuprofen, but that's just not in the cards, so I'm going to have to knuckle under and deal.

"So, am I just screwed? She's going to keep going after me every chance she gets? She orchestrated that whole thing so I'd run into her, then used that as an excuse to attack me. But thankfully the guards saw."

Sherese snorts indelicately and tosses a few stray braids over her shoulder. "Of course they did. Erin is as sneaky as a sledge-hammer. She barrels straight in and expects the fallout to fall her way. But that's not how things work down here. You have to use your brains, and your womanly assets. Win people over with a little sugar, and you'll go a lot further."

"Yeah, I'm not much for the *sugar*." I gesture down at my no-non-sense workout gear, which is holding up reasonably well so far to prison life. Though it's getting a little rank and could use a wash. I eye the sink, getting distracted from the conversation by the prospect of clean clothes.

"You could, you know. Manuel has a friend who's looking for a lady, and I'm sure if we fixed you up, you'd be his type. I've seen him checking you out, a time or two."

I blink a few times, completely appalled by the idea that one of the guards is into me, on *any* level. "I— I just can't." I finally stammer out something, so she'll drop the idea. I'm absolutely not sleeping with somebody for better food and a few cell perks. I'd rather be hungry, and wear the same clothes until I either die or get the heck out of here.

I wasn't sure how my first time would go, to be fair, but it certainly wasn't going to be with a creepy cult dude. *Hell no.*

"Give it some time, and think about it. You've got potential, fresh meat, and I'd hate to see you wither away in here and waste all my good efforts." She swings her legs up onto the cot, stretching out into a more comfortable position for a nap.

But I can't just let it go that quickly. I should, yes. She's extended the olive branch to me in a big way, answered my questions, and shared everything she has with me. I don't want to belittle that. And I know this is yet another way she's trying to help me, even though I'd rather die than give myself to a man in the Cabal like some sort of doll for his enjoyment.

"I can't do it, Sherese. I can't just lie down and die like that. I have to keep something for myself. Something to take out of this place."

She sighs, not offended, just weary. "Just think about it, Demy. I'm not saying it's the right way, but I've been down here a long, long time. And eventually . . . well, it's not lying down and dying. It's not. But if you let them think you have, you're going to last a lot longer."

With that, she pulls the pillow over her eyes to block out the lights, ending the conversation.

I match her pose, lying down on my back, and trying to find a position that doesn't make my arm injuries scream. But her words stick with me, and sleep doesn't come.

We aren't let out for dinner that evening, and I'm practically pacing by the time the door opens the next morning. Sherese doesn't get up from her cot, and it's not Manuel at the door. Our usual hall guard is back, his face grim.

He points to me. "Let's go."

"Just me?"

"Let's go!" he barks again, impatient today. I do as he says but cast a confused look over my shoulder at Sherese.

"Remember what I said," she calls just before the cell door is locked again. He leads me to a line of girls, this time with far more than just the new girls. It seems like every single woman has been pulled into the hall, except . . . Sherese, and the woman in blue. Nell is towards the back of the crowd, her blonde head only briefly visible before she's blocked again by a taller woman.

Unease sinks its claws into my back, and tension radiates through my whole body. This can't be good, whatever it is.

They lead us out, away from the holding area—my stomach rumbles, lamenting the lack of food, even if it does suck—and herd us into the halls. There are significantly more guards waiting on the other side of the metal gates, many of them leering in a way that makes my stomach lurch. I count the turns, and I'm pretty sure we're being led back to the medical exam room.

What the heck are they doing down here? Why are they bothering to feed us and keep us healthy? What's with all the trips to see the doctor?

There's no one to ask, of course, and I doubt they'd tell me if I tried with one of the guards. The nurse, Annie, might—but she could also write me off as a troublemaker, like Erin. I'm hungry and achy, and too stressed to make a good decision about what's a worthwhile risk.

So I stay silent, dread turning my limbs to stone as we're herded into the exam room, where both the doctor and Annie wait, clipboards in hand.

The guards all stay, forming up like sheepdogs, leaving us to be the livestock ripe for the plucking in the center. I search the crowd for Nell and spot her toward the back. I carefully weave through the other women to her side, and she grips my forearms, making me wince as pain shoots up my arms. I don't do anything except grip her back, cling to her like a lifeline in this strange and awful place.

We both scan the room warily, eyes dancing between the threatening guards and the terrifying medical staff.

"Idina, Brynne, Nell," Annie reads the names off the list, her voice flat and unconcerned. Nell's fingertips dig into me, a soft whimper breaking from her throat at the mention of her name. I tug her into my side, not caring if it paints a target on us. "Leigh, Starr, and Jen." Nobody moves for a heartbeat, and Annie's eyes snap up from the clipboard—annoyance the only readable emotion on her face.

She reads the list again, stopping to point at each woman. If they don't come out of the group willingly, one of the guards wades into the crowd to bodily take them out. Most go limp, but when her finger points at Nell, she stiffens in my arms.

"I can't, Demy. I can't. Whatever they're going to do, I just—"

"Don't fight, Nell. It's okay, it's going to be okay. We just have to stay alive, okay? You can do this. Look at me!" I shake her a little, but she screws her eyes shut and clings to me, burying her head in my neck.

Her sobs tear me in half as one of the men in black arrows toward us. He's got a lusty grin on his face, and I want to slap it off. I want to scream, to rage, to cry, to *fight*. Use that knowledge I worked so hard to gain with Peter and my guys—God, I hope Beckett is okay. And Fletcher. His deep brown eyes come to me in a flash, soothing as we lay on that roof together.

I hang onto that memory like a lifeline as Nell is snatched from my grip, her sobs surely cutting me deep enough to make me bleed. But she doesn't go willingly. She's crying, yes, but she strug-

66

gles in his grip. He has her by the upper arms, and shakes her roughly, like she's a naughty cat, not a grown woman. But she doesn't stop. Nell shoves her elbow back into his stomach with all the force she has, which elicits a half grunt. While he's distracted, she turns and flings up her knee, nailing him in the jewels.

He swears and drops her, clutching his privates and doubling over. But he doesn't stay bent for long, and there's nowhere for Nell to go, nowhere safe to hide in the panicked crowd. He backhands her as he straightens, so hard her small frame is knocked to the side. Women are trying to dodge, cowering away from the guard's erupting anger. I surge forward, trying to catch her before she tumbles all the way to the ground.

More guards are pressing forward, women are screaming—one of them might be me—as the guards push inward, compressing us into a tighter and tighter circle. The one sent in for Nell stomps forward, grabbing her by the hair and one arm, pulling her from the crowd. I try to push through, get to her, stop him, but the other women have squished further and further in, until I can't move, can't breathe. My thoughts are a panicked mess.

More and more women are dragged from the central group, until all of the exam tables are full. All of us are strapped down, and then the testing begins.

I close my eyes, scrunching them so tight my eyelids hurt and I can't see any of the women on the tables. And then I turn inward, begging my mind to take me away, anywhere but here.

Anywhere but here.

CHAPTER TWELVE

AN OFFER

DEMY

I'm curled on my side, staring at the wall. I haven't spoken, haven't washed since they dragged us out of our cells yesterday. It was more of the same—more blood draws—plus the added discomfort of a pelvic exam. This time, I was one of the women who also got ultrasounds. No one told us why, or what they were looking for.

But I just can't shake the malaise, the horrible feeling of *invasion*. And so I lie on my cot, and I stare at the wall. I briefly let myself wander all the way down the path of worry that maybe Beckett didn't *really* get out. Surely if he had, he'd have been able to lead Atlas and his security firm to find us. Right? So maybe he didn't make it out. The thought fills me with despair.

A wash rag appears in front of my eyes, damp and cool when Sherese lays it over my forehead.

"You can't give up, Demy. That's what they want. Docile sheep, to test and work over. But you're better than that."

"Not today, I'm not." The words are a sparse whisper, but I know she hears, because she huffs her annoyance at my attitude full of *quit.*

"You can have today. Take your time, mourn your losses. But tomorrow? I'll drag your scrawny tail out of that bed, and you won't stop me, or I'll feed you to the wolves." As she paces, her angry footsteps are loud thuds in our near-empty cell.

I don't argue. I just clutch my thin blanket a little closer to my chest and use the rag to wipe my eyes.

The next morning, Sherese shakes me awake. I don't argue, I just sit up and let my feet touch the ground for the first time since they dumped us back into our cells, and it feels a little strange. Like touching the ground means I'm back in the land of the living, and I'm not sure that I want to be.

"Wash, and brush your teeth." Her orders are firm but not unkind as she tidies a loose braid end.

I move stiffly, like a puppet, as I do her bidding. Slowly, I come back to myself. The numbness doesn't want to recede this time like it did before. It clings onto me like the watery grip of Davy Jones, risen from the pages of myth to drag me under the ocean of despair. I might not even notice if I drowned, if it consumed me.

But eventually, I'm as clean as I can be with only one set of dirty clothes, and my teeth are once again squeaky clean. I turn to face Sherese, who nods her approval.

"Please sit, I'd like to discuss something with you."

So formal. Is she kicking me out? Trading up for a less numbed-out roomie? I can't be the only zombie today.

"I want you to consider something. I know you're going to want to say no, but don't answer me yet. Think about it through breakfast and tell me when we're back inside our room. I'll handle the rest."

I stay quiet, not interested in any offer except *getting the hell out of here.*

"Manuel has a friend. His name is Lee, and he is looking for a lady friend. Manuel says he is very generous, and not abusive. I think if you treated him well enough, he would look after your short friend, as well."

My short friend. Nell. She would be ticked at being called short if we had the bandwidth to care about such trivial things right now.

"He will make himself known to you during breakfast. Whatever you do, do not insult the man. And then speak to me after, with your decision."

I nod, no words coming to explain to her how utterly repulsive I find the entire proposition without spitting on her offer of safety, in whatever form it comes.

A few short minutes later, the hall guard opens our door, offering us food for the first time in . . . two days? I follow Sherese, keeping my eyes on the floor. When we're inside the holding room, my legs move on instinct to carry me to the line for food, where all of the women are unusually subdued. There's no chatter, only the soft shuffle of feet on concrete floor, and the occasional sharp crack of plastic trays on the metal service window.

I'm handed my plate of beans and rice, today with half a banana and no meat, mystery or otherwise. I take it wordlessly, shuffling across the room to the tables. I take my usual seat next to Sherese, and then look up for Nell. My heart speeds when I realize I don't see her. I half-stand from the table, scanning over everyone's heads, looking for her short, blonde frame. My palms are sweating and I'm nearly in a panic when I finally spot her.

I abandon my tray and walk as quickly as I dare without drawing attention from the ever-looming guards. They're thankfully distracted right now, as one of the women has decided to make use of the open showers at the back of the room. I frown as I realize it's Erin, back from wherever they took her after her most recent strike. I avert my eyes as she strips to the cheering of the guards, focusing in on Nell and doing my best to block it all out.

She looks terrible. Her hair is a mess, and her face is black and blue, as are her arms. I have a feeling the rest of her isn't looking much better, but I can't see under her jeans and long-sleeved tee.

"Nell, oh my word, what happened?" I sink to my knees at her side, wanting to embrace her but not sure that I can touch her anywhere without causing pain.

Silent tears track down her cheeks, pain radiating off of her like a giant, throbbing wound. I scoot around so that I'm sitting next to her, with both our backs against the wall. Then carefully, as gently as I can, I wrap an arm around her shoulders.

Nell collapses into my side, shoulders heaving under the onslaught of pain and emotion. The tiny, domineering pixie I first met has vanished, nothing left that I remember except blue eyes and beat-up sneakers.

I hold her for a while, until the sobs slow to halting hiccups. My shirt is soaked, my skin sticky from her tears, but I just hold her, letting her feel whatever she needs to feel.

"Do you want to talk about it?" I ask, words barely audible in the oversized room.

She's silent for a few minutes more, and when the words do come, they're broken. "They're giving me shots of something, Demy. Atlas—" She chokes on another sob, even his name too painful a memory to drag into the ugly gray hell we find ourselves in. "He— We were finally ready. To try for kids. They keep scanning me, and now they're injecting me with something. What if it messes with me? Makes it so we can never . . ." She can't finish the sentence. "He won't want me anymore. Not if I can't do the one thing—" The confession is so heartbreaking, I forget her bruises and hold her tighter, trying to squeeze the horrible what-ifs out of her.

"Nell, you know that's not going to happen. We know what they're supposed to be doing down here, sure. But they haven't killed us. Haven't done anything—" I stop, unable to say they haven't hurt us, when she lies broken in my arms, and I'm only a half degree better. "Well, they've kept us relatively healthy, considering. Atlas loves you for *you*. He's stayed with you for years with no children. If, God forbid, something terrible happens down here and you can't have children, he won't stop loving you, Nell. He may never forgive himself, but I've seen the way that man looks at you. He would burn the whole world to ash if that's what it took to get you back. We just have to hang on until he finds us. He's private security. He literally *excels* at finding people, protecting. And that Glitch guy seemed pretty smart."

I stop and swallow, my own trauma responses making it hard to continue. Glitch had found things about me that I never knew, things that hurt. Surely he could find one creepy cult compound?

"The only thing that matters is staying alive, do you hear me?"

She shakes her head, refusing to meet my eyes.

"It's okay. It's okay to mourn, to regret what's happened. But Nell, I can't do this alone. I can't get us out of here without your help."

Nell sniffles but doesn't respond. Suggestions that we should eat are met with more stony silence.

So, I do the only thing I can. I hold her and pray to any God who'll listen that Atlas finds us soon.

When we're lining up to go back to our cells, a guard appears at my side. He's a few inches taller than me, and eyes me with an approving gaze. He's got pale skin—seemingly from genetics as well as his time in this sunless compound—and his eyes are a clear, icy blue. I haven't seen him before, because I would have noticed his eyes. He wordlessly offers me a banana. Shiny and whole, it doesn't even have any brown spots on it yet. Unlike the half banana already on my plate, which was a bit mushy looking. Not that I got to eat any of it, my stomach chooses that moment to rumble and remind me.

"You didn't eat," he says, grabbing my wrist. He turns my hand over and presses it into my palm. The touch is gentle, yet firm. Somehow, despite the lack of force, the clammy touch makes my skin crawl.

Lee.

I'd completely forgotten he was going to be *making himself known* as Sherese put it, since Nell took my complete focus.

But here he is, standing in front of me, waiting for something. And I realize I have to make a call, right here and now. Sherese had said to tell her, but Lee isn't walking away. And while I'm utterly repulsed by the man, Nell's broken sobs are branded into my soul. I know what I have to do, even as pinpricks of revulsion circle my wrist where his hand lingers on me.

"Thank you, Lee." I force myself to smile, and slowly lift my hand with the banana, freeing it from his grip. I crack open the top of the peel, and make eye contact as I take a small bite.

A grin cracks his face, and somehow it makes things better, not worse. He's less of a brainwashed cult sycophant for a moment, and more of a regular man, trying to impress a woman. He gives me a sharp nod, then walks away, back to whatever post he abandoned to bring me his gift.

The fact that I've stained my soul with that one small bite doesn't matter. What matters is another chance to learn more, see other parts of this compound, and hopefully find a way to escape before Nell shatters beyond repair.

And to save her light, I'll bear whatever sins, whatever stains it takes. I've lived through worse, and as I slowly eat the banana on the way back to my cell, I make myself a vow.

I'll live through this too, so I can burn it to the ground.

Atlas isn't the only one with a temper.

CHAPTER THIRTEEN

ROOM AND BOARD

ATLAS

I snatch open the boardroom door, ignoring the yammering assistant in the expensive dress.

"Sir, Mr. Vaughn is *not* receiving right now. I insist you come with me, or else I'll call security!"

"You do that," I murmur as I stride into the room, Glitch and Fletcher on my heels. Glitch I'm used to. He's a nattering but useful presence, and over the years I've grown fond of the guy. Fletcher, however, I didn't see coming. A blind spot, one that smarts given my utter failure to protect my wife. But no matter how many times I shove him back, he keeps pressing forward.

I'd respect it if I cared about anything right now.

The door hits the wall loudly and bounces back to my outstretched hand. Every head in the room turns, each person clad in a power suit and a matching sneer. I don't care how powerful they *think* they are; all I care about is getting my wife back.

Adam Vaughn stands at the head of the table, clad in a navy suit with a buttoned vest and steel-gray patterned tie underneath that matches the salt in his hair and the steely gaze he's leveled on me. He's stopped mid-stream from his monologue by our entrance.

"I think you've wandered into the wrong board room." He flicks a finger at one of his c-suite members. "Get security."

The woman in a red pantsuit hurries to comply, quickly lifting the conference phone in the middle of the mahogany desk. I cast a quick look at Glitch, whose fingers are already flying.

"The line's dead, sir. I—"

Glitch looks up, no smugness, despite the fact that I know he's the one who's killed the phones in the entire building in three seconds flat. The man travels prepared for all contingencies.

"I need a word with you, Vaughn." I jerk my thumb towards the door.

"This is a board meeting, Pacelli. I won't have you waltzing in off the street and dragging me out—"

Good, he's done his research. He knows who I am and why I'm here. "Let me stop you right there. You want to talk about your son's *ransom* and kidnapping in front of all your employees, we can. Word spreads when you pay cults to get your heir back. The choice is yours, but we *will* be having a conversation."

"Where is security!" he bellows, face turning red over his expensive tie.

"Stuck on an elevator," Glitch answers helpfully, pushing his glasses up his nose. He looks so innocent, but he really gets up to whatever he wants. A fact I find particularly useful right at this moment.

"Everyone, out!" he barks, losing some of his bluster now that he realizes we've suborned his security, and help is not on the way to roust us.

Flustered executives shoot us death glares as they gather up their folios and projections, skirting us widely as they file out.

"What is the meaning of this?" Vaughn snaps as soon as the door clicks shut behind the last employee.

"You know exactly what this is about," I say with a calm I don't feel. "You paid a ransom and got your son out of the Cabal's headquarters. I need to know who you contacted, and every other detail you can give us so we can retrieve the two women you left behind in there, one of whom was your son's match. Not that you care, clearly."

He stares at me without a shred of remorse, looking down his aquiline nose at me. "Yes, yes I did ransom my son, a fact that I would have preferred not become common knowledge," he says with a glare, dropping both palms on the end of his conference table. "They delivered a burner phone to my mail room in broad daylight, and then vanished into thin air. The line is dead now, so you're barking up a dead tree. Now get the hell out of my conference room."

"No. You will tell us everything you know about the Cabal, or I'll have you arrested. Glitch here might be able to trace the phone."

"On what authority?" he scoffs. "You're a trumped-up body-guard, with no power whatsoever. Even if you were with the police, it's not illegal to pay a ransom."

The door flies open again, and a huffing, puffing pregnant Queen Sadie storms through the door.

"On my authority, Mr. Vaughn. And I think it's past time we were introduced."

A very concerned Faith, her sister in law, trails her in the door, looking nervously at her surroundings.

"What are you doing here, Sadie?" I ask, briefly diverting from the main point.

"Glitch told me what was going on, and I decided to lend a hand," Sadie declares, lifting her chin and daring me to contradict her. Faith pulls out the leather, high-backed chair at the end of the conference table, and gestures for Sadie to sit.

Sadie ignores her.

She may be pregnant and short of breath, wearing maternity jeans and a sweater, but in that moment, she looks at each of us with every bit of power and dignity that accompanies her title as queen. A wiser man would have taken the hint, but Vaughn isn't wise. Only arrogant. He glares at her, an insolent smirk twisting his lips.

He scoffs as Faith leans in toward Sadie's ear and whispers, "Sadie, you're supposed to be sitting down. Patrick is going to be *very* unhappy with us if he finds out you're up and about against doctor's orders."

She settles her small frame gracefully into the oversized executive chair, not bothered by Vaughn's scrutiny. Faith hovers at her shoulder, a mother hen with an unruly chick.

"And what do you think you're going to do, little girl, that the men in this room haven't accomplished?" Vaughn asks, waving imperiously at the three of us, standing with our arms crossed at the side of the room.

"Oh, I don't know. Call the head of the NAA Police and his best interrogator. Call my husband. Oh, ooh, I like this one better. I'm going to personally give Atlas the green light to throw your sorry hide in jail until you decide to stop obstructing our investigation." There's steel in her eyes as she stares him down. But he doesn't take the hint.

I step up to her side, lending my support, and Fletcher mirrors my action, stepping up to her other side.

"He doesn't seem to believe me, Atlas. Perhaps I should just call the tax investigation department. In a business this size, I'm sure there have been a few accounting errors over the years. I've got twelve *very* bored accountants just itching for a new project. Don't you think that Vaughn Family Capital Holdings would be an excellent candidate?"

"Sounds as good a job as any," I murmur, trying not to come undone at the normally sweet woman's willingness to do literally anything to get people back that she considers to be in her care.

My gut tightens at the painful reminder of why she's dragged herself here.

Vaughn scoffs at her threats, but I can see when the penny drops, and recognition dawns. She's not wearing her crown, or a luxurious ball gown. None of the frivolous adornments she uses for TV appearances. But she's every inch the queen even in faded denim and a ponytail, and something in the man's facade crumbles at the edges when he finally recognizes her.

He leans forward, pressing a button on the conference phone. Silence is the only greeting for a second, and he looks accusingly up at the five of us.

"Uh, hang on," Glitch says, red tingeing the tips of his ears as he swipes at his tablet.

The dial tone returns, and then his assistant's harassed voice comes over the speaker. "Yes, Mr. Vaughn?"

"Bring Beckett." He jabs the button to close the line, not bothering with any niceties.

In less than two minutes, a haggard-looking Beckett walks into the room, flanked by two beefy guards with *security* emblazoned across their tight, black t-shirts.

Amateurs.

"Hello," Beckett says lightly, before dropping into a chair in the middle of the long table, midway between his glaring father and the rest of us. "Any luck on locating the women?" he at least has the good grace to ask, but it only sends my rage into a fever pitch.

"You know damn well we haven't found them, or we wouldn't be here dealing with your imbecile of a father and his horde of sycophantic bootlickers. We need to know everything you can remember about where you were taken, and how far they drove after you were taken from their compound. Every single detail. Anything could be the clue we need to tip them off, and your father cares more about power games and appearances than he does about innocent lives."

Beckett levels a disappointed look at his father and rubs a weary hand over his forehead.

"They kept us drugged any time we were in transit, so I'm afraid I don't know much about how far we were taken. They used black SUVs, which I'm sure you already know."

I nod, frustration building up inside me to the point I feel like a volcano ready to erupt. "We found them, abandoned in Southern New Texas in a farmer's back forty."

"Huh. New Texas. I wouldn't have guessed, but . . . yeah. When I came to, they booted me out of the SUV on the side of the road, with a burner phone programmed with my father's number."

"Do you still have the phone?" Glitch interrupted, eager to get his hands on any tech that belonged to the Cabal.

"Yeah, can one of you go grab it?" Beckett asks his guards. One of them walks out immediately, and the tension between my shoulders eases a bit.

"Grab the other one too, please," Glitch interjects again, sliding into a chair, and pulling a pair of cords out of his messenger bag, then hooking them to his tablet.

We're going to find her. She has to be okay. I shove down the worries for my wife, focusing on the task at hand.

"What else do you remember?"

"Everything was flat, and it was dark. Dad would probably be able to pinpoint the exact location better than I would since he sent the helicopter to pick me up."

I swivel my gaze toward the elder Vaughn.

"We don't have all day, man. She's having contractions, and I need to get her back to the hotel," Faith snaps, surprising me. The woman was so timid when I met her, she wouldn't make eye contact. Now, she's standing her ground with ease.

Clearly, marriage to Teddy all these years has agreed with her.

"They're Braxton-Hicks, Faith." Sadie waves her worried sister down, but I can see the tightness in her jaw, now that I'm paying attention.

Hell. The last thing I need is Sadie going into premature labor on our watch.

"Do you have a driver downstairs?"

"Yes, we do."

"You can go. I appreciate you coming, but I think that both Vaughns now realize it's in their best interest to cooperate with us."

Sadie stands slowly, barely concealing a grimace as she clutches the side of her stomach. "Atlas, I expect a full report as soon as you leave here. If his cooperation is any less than *one hundred percent*, you have my full authority to arrest him, his son, and anyone who tries to stop you. Peter should be here anytime—"

The man in question slams through the door, a frustrated glare pinned on his stubborn younger sister. "Sadie! Patrick is climbing the walls looking for you," he scolds, gently taking her arm and shooting an exasperated look at Faith.

"Don't look at me—you know how stubborn she is!" Faith says, leading Sadie toward the door.

"Let's go, then. Patrick said something about the doctor putting her on bed rest."

"I can hear you two, you know. And I'm pregnant, not dead," she grouses as they lead her out.

"Yes, and we'd like to keep you *not dead*," Faith chides as their voices are muffled by the door closing behind them.

"You people are like a circus, and I'm supposed to respect the heads of this country?" Adam Vaughn is still pissy, arms crossed over his chest indignantly.

"That would be wise. Now, I need a location, and I need it ten minutes ago." I level a hard glare on the man.

He rattles off a set of coordinates by memory, the guard returns with the cell phones, and the three of us are out the door at top speed.

We finally have a lead on Nell's location, and nothing is going to stop me from getting to her.

CHAPTER FOURTEEN

SHOCKWAVE

DEMY

"**E**verybody on your feet! Right now, let's move!" The booming masculine yell startles me awake, along with the slamming open of our cell door. I roll off the bed but catch myself in a push-up position, barely able to blink the sleep from my eyes before calloused hands are dragging me up, off the floor and into the hallway. The overhead lights are still dim. Sleep-tousled women are hanging onto each other, some crying, as we're shoved gracelessly into the halls by the Cabal men. Even Sherese, normally exempt from this kind of unpleasantry, is shoved so hard she stumbles into my back. I steady her as I scan the crowd for Nell.

She's so petite that it's hard to spot her in the terrorized crowd, but eventually I do. She's pressed back against the bars, her face white with terror.

"Nell!" I muscle through the crowd, ignoring Sherese's warning hiss. When I reach her I form a human shield, placing myself between her and the rest of the terrified crowd trying to get as far from the guards as possible. We didn't make it this far to get trampled in a hallway.

Within minutes, the hall is packed to bursting and the cells are empty. The lead guard opens the gate out into the main part of the compound, and the horde is moving. I wait for an opening and take it, pulling Nell along with me. I don't let go of her hand, because I can't risk us getting separated again, whatever is going on.

Her hand is shaking in mine, but we press forward, herded by screaming guards and the occasional shove. There is no way to tell what's happening. No fire alarms, or crazy lights like when we were under attack at the NLC, and yet the place teems like someone kicked an anthill.

More men in black than I've ever seen are everywhere; running, shouting, cursing. We're funneled like cattle through a narrow hallway, and fear climbs the back of my throat as we're pushed towards empty blackness ahead. The lights are out, and deep, biological fear of the dark threatens to choke me.

Are they going to kill us now? That's what we've always heard. The Cabal experiments on you, then wipes you out. This may be it.

I grip Nell's hand tighter. I may not know what's ahead, but I'm going to either make it out or go down swinging, and I'm not leaving her behind.

We enter the unlit portion of the hall, terrified whimpers and sobs the only thing breaking the complete darkness.

All my old nightmares come rushing back in a crushing weight on my chest. I freeze; suddenly I'm the scared kid hiding behind a dumpster in a pitch-black alley, the fetid stench of rot and the heat of my own breath on my face as I cry silently, praying the scary man doesn't find me, and snatch me out to kill me.

He didn't then. But now I know how much worse it is than I always feared, and it's near-crippling.

"Demy, we can't stay here," Nell whispers, shaking my shoulders. I've been brushed to the side of the hall by the steady stream of bodies, and I squinch my eyes tightly shut.

I can't. I *can't.*

"Demy!" Nell's tone is sharp, and I crack my eyes open. "I know it's awful, and I know it's scary—" her voice breaks. "But we're almost at the back, and we don't want to be the closest to the guards. They've got batons. Please, we have to keep moving. Please," she says, shaking me again. "Just one foot in front of the other. You've been strong for me, let me be strong for you."

I lurch forward, like a stalled engine jolting back to life. I can see the relief in her eyes as she drags me into the stream of humanity.

The dark feels like it's swallowing me whole, consuming every bit of me that's left. My breath comes in painful, shallow huffs. I can't see the back of her head anymore, and if we didn't have a death grip on each other, I'd feel like I'd been lost to the deep of space, a black hole of nothing.

Nell's presence is the only thing that keeps me moving. Because if I stop now, if I lose my grip, I'll be alone.

And I don't want to be alone, I realize. More than anything I've ever wanted before, I'm sick to death of being alone and afraid.

I move faster, spurred on by the realization. We're jogging blindly now, trying to get space between us and the looming threat of the guards behind us. Whatever's ahead can't be worse than they are.

The ground under our feet changes, tilting slightly upward. A breath of cold, damp air hits my face, and realization clicks in my subconscious.

The darkness shifts subtly, taking on a velvet quality as we keep climbing the ramp. When I breathe in the scent of pines, I realize what's been missing since we got here.

Dew-kissed grass squishes under my shoes, lending a chill to my already shaking form. *Outside.* The moon is just a sliver overhead, but it's enough to see the truth behind us.

We've been underground. No windows. No exits. No fresh air, or breeze.

Their compounds are underground.

This could be exactly what Atlas and his team need to find us, but how can we tell them? There are guards already waiting, forming a human net as they herd us towards large, enclosed transport trucks. There are two waiting, with ramps down as women are being urged into the backs. My throat nearly sticks shut at the idea of being back inside a completely dark enclosed space.

I'm moving woodenly, dread slowing my movements, when a hand grabs my arm and snatches me to the side so hard it rips Nell's hand from my grip.

I scream, the sound ripped from my throat, before being silenced by a clammy hand over my mouth.

"Shh, it's me."

It takes two long beats for me to recognize the voice, and I don't know whether to be more or less afraid in Lee's grip.

I bat his hand away from my mouth.

"Nell! Please, let us stay together." I sound hysterical. I know it, he knows it, and there's not a dang thing I can do about it.

"Stay with Rich and I'll get her," he orders, passing me off to a friend like the plaything he sees me as.

Beefy arms wrap around my chest, locking me against Rich's body as Lee darts into the darkness.

My breathing has shallowed out again, and I feel lightheaded by the time he returns with a wide-eyed and terrified Nell.

"Nell!" I manage the word, though it's like there's no air behind it. She stops fighting Lee when she sees me, running toward me instead.

"You two are riding with us. But you've got to stay quiet," he chides, as if I'm a naughty child.

I want to punch him. I want to spit in his face, and kick him in the jewels. But there's a cold math to captivity, and I'm seeing it more by the minute.

Fighting means going into the dark box truck. Fighting means pain, and abuse. Fighting means a horde of angry men to escape from. But two of us against two of them yields much better odds.

So, I don't scream, or fight, or spit in Lee's smug face. I offer him my hand and follow him into the night.

Chapter Fifteen

EMPTY

Atlas

We don't take a chopper this time—Patrick insists. He makes a few calls, and as soon as we are out of the boardroom, he sends us coordinates to a landing strip a few miles away.

A military transport plane is waiting for us, turbine engines already running. We park our SUV right on the tarmac. There are two pilots standing at the stairs to greet us.

"Atlas, nice to see you again." The female pilot steps forward to shake my hand. It takes me a moment to place her, between the flight suit and the tight bun, but when I do, my eyes widen.

"Jenna? And is that Marcus?" My gaze skips over to the second pilot, a few years her senior, and also familiar.

"Yes, sir. I hear they took Nell. We're here to help you get her back."

Tears sting my eyes.

"Care to make introductions?" Fletcher asks.

"Fletcher, Glitch, this is Jenna and Marcus. They were matched the same year as Nell and I. But I haven't seen them since we left for Mairmont all those years ago. Jenna wanted to be a pilot, but I didn't know she'd gotten a waiver, too."

Jenna grinned wide. "After I heard about Nell getting to go to med school, I made a few calls. I was already pregnant by then, but Patrick was able to work it out for me. My mom lives on base and watches our son while we work. She's actually running childcare for several of the NAA Police families now as part of a new program."

"We'll be happy to tell you all about it once you're inside," another voice calls from the door of the plane. Patrick. He's impatient, but I'm surprised he's here at all. "We don't know how much time we have before this tip goes stale."

He's right. I don't waste any more time, jogging up the steps into the oversized aircraft. To my surprise, he's pulled out all the stops. There are NAA Police strapped into nearly every harness, weapons resting over their knees, faces serious.

Marcus is already sealing the door behind us, and Patrick points us to a section of open harnesses, the last on the plane.

Jenna's voice comes over the speakers. "Final call. Take off in ninety seconds. Fasten your harnesses for lift-off or get ready to eat the deck, because we're about to kick the tires and light the fires."

Glitch splutters as he fumbles the clips into his harness, and I see he's wedged his messenger bag in with him. Always about the technology, that one.

I unclip quickly to help him de-tangle, before settling into my own harness and cinching the straps down. It's not my favorite way to fly, but as I look around at the dozens of ready soldiers, and some of my closest friends who've shown up to help, a deep gratefulness settles into my bones.

Then one of the pilots is apparently done kicking the tires and lighting the fires—whatever the heck *that* means—because my stomach drops as we take flight. The sound of air hissing and afterburners blazing drowns out everything else.

There's no runway to land on, but there is a big, open farm road. Jenna and Marcus set us down on it with expert ease, even if it is a bumpy landing with the many potholes the aircraft is too big to dodge. We file off the plane quickly, and, without me having to say a word, the police are formed into squads and start patrolling.

Fletcher lets out a grunt of displeasure as he scans the rural area. "This looks completely deserted. We have no idea how far they could have driven to drop him here, either."

"No, but hopefully the patrols will find a clue." Shouts are already breaking the still afternoon as they call out findings to each other. Most are minor or calls of "clear," but one catches my attention.

"South-bound tire tracks! Fresh, less than thirty-six hours estimated!"

I break into a jog, towards the squad who called it out, with Fletcher hot on my heels. I have to see it with my own eyes.

Sure enough, there's flattened sedge grass and a few deeper ruts, as if a large, heavy vehicle got stuck briefly in a patch of wet clay. They lead due south, before disappearing into the wavy, wild plains grasses.

"Requesting drones," one of the officers calls and, within a minute flat, I hear the buzz of propellers zooming past overhead.

Fletcher and I exchange a glance, before breaking into a ground-eating jog after the mini-copters.

The squadron of police follow us on foot, not complaining about the pace we set.

"What are we looking for?" Fletcher asks, eyes trained to the ground even as he runs.

"Anything that doesn't belong. Tracks, buildings, relay towers, signs of technology or deliveries; we won't know until we find it."

He nods, and falls quiet.

We jog a mile, then another, before the crack of a large-caliber bullet piercing the air has us all dropping to the ground, flat on our stomachs.

I watch as one of the drones up ahead spirals into a crash, bits of plastic and metal flying into the air as it slams into the trunk of a tree. There's no other movement, no sign of humanity, but *someone* is here. I rise to a careful crouch, lifting my pistol from its holster on my side. I give a hand signal for everyone to move forward but stay low.

We move as one silent entity, the squadron fanning out behind me to cover more ground. Fletcher pulls his own handgun out and follows on my six. Gunfire rips through the air again, downing the second drone, in roughly the same spot as the other. But this time I'm watching, and I see where the bullet comes from.

"Eleven o'clock!" I bark the warning, then head straight for the source, keeping low so my approach is obscured by the waving grasses.

A hundred yards later, I stop, observing the camouflaged tower which shot it down. Crouching down, I find a pebble on the ground, and toss it towards the base of the tower.

Nothing.

I repeat the action, this time tossing it as high up in the air as I can, in a broad arc past the tower. It responds, a mounted gun on top swiveling and blasting the tiny pebble into smithereens.

A few more pebbles confirm my suspicion. I give a hold signal, then radio Glitch.

"We've got an anti-aircraft weapon. Can you assess and disable it remotely, and tell me if the control is local or long distance?"

"Sure thing—hold for a moment," he says, chipper at having a task. "Huh. I don't see any network evidence of anything, even with my . . . less than legal scanners. Which means it's likely hardwired to a local network."

"So it has to be disabled manually?"

He hesitates. "Err . . . yes?"

"Okay. See you soon. Ask Patrick if there's any body armor in the plane before you come."

I cut the comm, not bothering to wait and listen to him splutter. I need him moving, and quickly. The Cabal is close, I can *feel* it. And every second we waste, is a second they could be hurting my wife, and Demy.

I bolt wide left, sticking to the cover of the grasses and staying low. The tower doesn't move, but I don't stop, don't slow until I'm well past the range it took aim at the aircraft.

But that's not what stops me. It's the deep, rutted tire tracks—like a large number of vehicles left the area recently—which halts me mid-stride.

A feeling of dread consumes me, eating away at my soul as I stare at the evidence that we're probably too late. I hear the criticism in my father's voice, mocking and a little slurred from overindulgence in his favorite bourbon.

Too late. Not enough. Not going to ever get her back. You didn't deserve her, anyway.

But I can't dwell in that space. I can't be this close to finding her, and let myself miss her because my head was in the past. So, I shut down my emotions, shut down everything that makes me a great husband, and a hopeful father. The process of shutting it all out is oddly calming, and there's only one thing left inside me when I'm done.

A white-hot flame of rage, fueled by the promise of vengeance against whoever took Nell.

Chapter Sixteen

FLUSHED

Demy

We drive for a long time. Nell and I are in the front seat of a supply truck much like the old military vehicles sometimes still used by the NAA Police, the back full of equipment from the bunker, covered in nondescript canvas. Nobody will look twice at us, and as we pass through multiple populated areas, everything in me is screaming to signal for help. But Lee sits in the passenger seat, next to the rolled-up window, and in the driver's seat is his friend, Rich.

The bench seat is deep but wasn't made for four people. Even with how petite Nell is, we're wedged in hip-to-hip, and I'm pointedly ignoring Lee's hand resting on my knee. He hasn't moved it, hasn't tried anything more, but it feels like a test. Will I allow him this because of his *special treatment* in letting us stay out of the box truck?

As much as it makes my skin crawl, I do. Because I've realized something as we drive through all these little towns full of people. My opportunity won't be in the bunker, or whatever prison they take us to next.

My opportunity is convincing Lee to take us *out* of the bunker, even if just into the woods. If I could make it to any small town, I could hide like a pro, and get the word out to Atlas and his team. Once they know what they're looking for, I have no doubt they'll be able to find the rest of the Cabal.

So, I watch, keeping vigilant count of which towns we pass through and in which order. The position of the sun in the sky, telling me which direction we're heading.

All the while, I ignore his palm on my knee.

Nell remains silent but strong at my side, her bruises' green-yellow tint even more pronounced in the bright light of day.

Eventually we turn off the main roads, bumping through the transition from pristine pavement to the older, more crumbled roads that don't see maintenance. Which means this is a wild area, where no one lives anymore. When the NAA shrunk into tri-states, vast swaths of suburban development were abandoned, some closed and ready to be used later, but others were left to go back to nature.

The longer we drive, the more I'm convinced that this is the latter. I stare out the window, watching the old subdivisions pass by, silent sentries covered in vines, some with trees growing through the roofs. A few aren't recognizable as old dwellings at all, except for the fact that the plants are higher, and the 'hill' is uneven and bumpy, meaning the foliage has closed over short buildings.

It's oddly soothing, and I let my mind wander as I watch. Which is why some time later, when the truck slows to a bumping stop, I'm surprised to see that we're at a fully functional waystation.

Gas pumps, larger diesel pumps for semitrucks, and a shining, glass-front store look completely out of place cut from the abundant wilderness. There is a small office park across the street, and a handful of warehouses dotted along the full length of the highway, but any residences that used to be here have been overgrown and taken back to nature. It's the crystallized juxtaposition between what society *was* and *is*.

Rich puts the truck into park and cracks his back with an overhead stretch that has Nell flinching away from his protruding elbows.

"Are we just fueling up?" I ask, spying regular-looking people walking from cars to the station.

Lee smiles, the look genuine and accompanied by a knee squeeze. "That, and we thought you ladies might need to use the facilities." He lifts his hand from my knee, and jerks his thumb toward the gleaming service station, and I have to stop the urge to swallow hard.

I keep my face a blank smile, nodding. "That would be great, thank you."

He gives me a jovial grin as he cracks the door open, but pauses, hand still on the truck frame, boxing me in. "Don't try to run off, now. I'd hate to have to chase you down." He chucks my chin with his thumb, and a cold chill runs down my spine. Because the words may have been jovial, but the threat in his icy eyes is *very* real.

"Of course not. Right, Nell?" I murmur, reaching a hand back for hers. She clasps my palm in a death grip.

"Wouldn't dream of it," she agrees, managing to sound breezy, all the while her fingernails are digging into my palm with repressed rage.

"Good. Let's go." He hops down from the tall cab of the truck, and extends both hands to me, like a child he's going to lift down. I force myself to let my palms meet his and accept the wholly unnecessary touch. I don't cringe from the contact—at least not

96

on the outside. My leg still feels heavy where his hand rested, as if the weight of him is burned into my flesh after so many hours, and I know that as soon as I'm locked into a bathroom stall alone, I'm going to scrub at the area, scratch it, wash it . . . anything to make the feeling go away. To remove the taint he's left on my skin, even though he's only touched the knee of my pants.

He keeps hold of my hand, twining our fingers together as if we're lovers, and I let him. I hate myself for it, but I let him. Because in my other hand is Nell's, and we have to work together to get out of this mess.

The deeper we get, the less I want to wait for someone to come along and rescue us. But my mind is also searching for any way to leave a message, if not to break free. Inside, the store is full of racks of pristine goods. Fresh sandwiches and cut fruit have my mouth watering, while bags of salty chips look like a treat from above.

I've got no access to my money, though, and I'm not willing to ask for anything that might be considered a favor or might oblige me to reciprocate further.

But the first thing I eat when I get free of these sadists? It's going to be a salty vat of potato chips bigger than my entire torso.

Lee doesn't let go of my hand until I'm standing at the door to the women's bathroom. I'm not surprised to see it's an individual stall; a larger, multi-stall bathroom would have allowed us to speak to someone, or borrow a phone in privacy to call nine-one-one.

No, instead, he sticks his head in and checks that it's empty, before waving us both to go in. Then, he leans against the wall, directly outside. The message is clear; the privacy is an illusion.

I give him a smile that I hope doesn't look as fake as it feels, before opening the door and sliding in. Nell follows on my heels and locks the door with a sigh of relief. But she doesn't stay there.

She goes straight to the toilet, and rips the lid off the back of the tank.

"What are you doing?" I whisper-hiss, casting a nervous glance at the door.

"Shh, look around for anything sharp. Anything loose," she orders, staring down into the tank, like it contains the secrets to life.

"There's nothing in here but paper towels. Even the soap dispenser and trash are built into the wall."

"Okay. We'll just have to make do. Do you need to go?"

"Uh, yes. Don't you?"

"Yeah. Just don't flush until after we both go. He'll get suspicious if we do more than twice."

"Err . . . okay," I murmur, confused. I do as she says, though, hurrying to go and then getting out of the way. She flushes when we're both done, then starts messing with things inside the tank.

"I'll tell you everything later, okay? How much longer do you think we have until he gets suspicious?" she asks when I'm done washing my hands.

"Another minute; two tops."

"That should be enough. Come on, come on! I might need your help." She jerks her head, urging me to come over. She's bending one of the metal poles that keeps the stopper flat. The rubber ball piece is already crooked, pointing towards the sky. Though I admit I'm not a plumber, I'm not clear on why she's breaking the toilet. "Put your hands right above mine and pull to the right."

I do as she asks, and after a few seconds, it starts to give.

"Stop! That's enough. I just wish we had something sharp, so I could carve a message in here."

Realization strikes.

"Would this work?" I pull my only remaining ruby earring out of my pocket, and she grabs it, bending to carve something into the tank as best she can. Most of our things were taken, but the earring was apparently trivial enough not to bother with during our abduction, despite its inherent value. But the metal stud protruding from the back might be enough to scratch the tank.

An impatient knock comes at the door. "Hurry it up, ladies! Unless of course you *want* me to come in there," Lee taunts. "In that case, take your time." He drums the door lightly with his fingertips, and it's like he's drumming directly on my spine, sending fear skittering through my nerves. I shudder as Nell quickly puts the lid back on and flushes it.

She does the fastest hand wash I've ever seen, and then we're out.

Lee looks disappointed but proffers his hand without comment. We walk back out into the sunlight, and it's only as we're loading into the truck that I realize Nell didn't give my earring back.

CHAPTER SEVENTEEN

BREAKDOWN

ATLAS

The tire tracks lead us to scuffed-up grass which covers an underground entrance. It takes a lot of digging and calling in a specialty piece of breaching equipment—which takes hours, and probably a millimeter off my back molars from all the grinding I do—but eventually they pop it open like a tin can, and we're in.

The sunken halls are deserted, but the power's on and we find food, clothing, and other evidence of recent occupation.

It's when we reach the security room, though, that I start to break down, cracks forming in my carefully erected shield. There are hours and hours of footage to dig through, but it takes barely minutes of review before we spot our girls. Nell was here, and I missed her by *hours*. Demy too. Fletcher is next to me, white knuckles gripping the back of a chair, eyes glued to the screen and a pissed-off expression on his face.

"I don't know how much more of this I can watch," he eventually says, rubbing his eyes wearily. It's late, and we're all tired.

It's still grinding my gears that we've got no idea how they were tipped off. They left before we hit their tower, or else we'd have seen the escape vehicles. And everyone at the elder Vaughn's company is now stonily silent, hiding behind their overzealous legal bulldogs.

"You don't have to," Patrick says, resting a hand on his shoulder. "We have police analysts who are going to go over every second for clues." He drops a hand on my shoulder as well, and only long familiarity keeps me from flinching away from the contact. I don't deserve comfort, not while my wife is being used and abused.

I change the view, flipping through cameras until we're following the women as they're herded through these same hallways to what looks like a poor mockery of an NLC medical center. Every muscle in my body tenses, as if it knows what I'm about to see before my brain has caught up.

The tattered curtains are never used, and then before my eyes, women are dragged from the terrified crowd, and start getting physically strapped to the exam tables. It takes less than a second to spot my wife, even though she's one of the smallest in the room.

Because she's fighting. The guard came to pluck her out, and she didn't go down easy. Pride is half strangled in my chest by horror as I see the much larger man in Cabal black attack her, and when he backhands her, I stand up so fast I knock the chair over.

"Turn it off." Patrick points at Glitch, who makes the disturbing images disappear in a few swipes of his tablet.

But the tremors in my muscles, the fury, the desire to go out and find that man and rip his head off his shoulders with my bare hands for daring to *breathe* near my wife, let alone hurt her—they don't care that it's off. The image is seared into my brain, and I know I'll see that proof of my failure to protect her every day for the rest of my life.

An animal sound rips itself from my throat. All the pain, all the rage, all the helpless impotence are wrapped into it. My throat is raw from it.

We were only hours behind them. *Hours.* And she's gone. Again. They've got her. They're beating her. My beautiful, spunky, loud-mouthed, and utterly perfect Nell.

My everything. My love who I swore I'd protect and never let go back to the days of abuse and terror she suffered as a child at the hands of her abusive family.

I've failed her.

And I'm never going to forgive myself.

Chapter Eighteen

Hollow

Demy

The end of our journey finds us at another underground bunker. Dread claws at my throat as Lee escorts Nell and me down, down, down, back into the bowels of the earth.

The sunshine, for the brief time we had it, breathed new life into me. Giving it up now feels like a little slice of death, delivered early. But this is a chance I never dreamed I'd have, so I do my best to memorize every set of steps, every turn from the exit to our new cells. And he takes us *straight* to the cells.

The setup is a little different in this bunker—there is no divider separating our cells from the ones across the walkway, and it appears there are fewer barriers overall. We walk down the row, and there are several cells with three women each, even though there are still only two cots.

When he stops, it's at Sherese's cell, and I'm relieved to see it's just her in there. Her usual orange dress is gone, though. Now she wears vibrant yellow, in a shorter style. It's every bit as clingy, but she wears it with grace.

"Only one here. Who's going in?" Lee asks with the door propped open.

"Demy, come," Sherese says without hesitation. I resist the urge to hug Nell, giving her a curt nod instead—but I hold her eyes, will her to stay strong. She holds mine right back, and the firm set of her shoulders tells me she's okay, for now at least.

Lee's trickier. Do I hug him? Shake his hand? It's a sick contemplation, figuring out how to *thank* my jailer. But I have to keep on his good side, or my opportunity goes away.

It feels like another test, but he takes matters into his own hands before I can decide. He leans forward, closing the distance between us.

I can feel his breath hot on my cheek as he whispers in my ear, "Thanks for keeping me company today. We should do it again soon, but just the two of us." He lets one finger trail down my neck, and it lingers on my collarbone suggestively.

Goosebumps pop up on the back of my arms, and my heart is pounding like I'm fighting hand-to-hand. I want to slap away the touch. But I force myself to stay still, keep my expression pleasant.

Pleasant might be a stretch. *Neutral* is the best I hope I accomplish. Finally, it hits me.

"It was much better riding with you than in the back of that awful truck," I murmur, keeping my voice low.

A grin splits his face, showing off his teeth. They're straight and white enough, but still the wolfish expression sends a shiver of unease through me.

"Yeah it was," he says, like he's awarded me a great prize. Masculine pride oozes from him as he waves me into the cell and locks me away.

I watch as he leads Nell down the hall to another cell, trying desperately not to cry, or think about the little chips of my soul I'm breaking off and selling to stay alive.

They don't feed us that night, which is why I'm still awake when there's a scuffle in the hall in the wee hours of the night. I roll to my stomach—ignoring its angry growls—and lift my head just enough to see over the edge of my cot, without making it obvious that I'm awake.

Sherese is still breathing the deep, even breaths of sleep, but if she were awake, she would scold me to mind my own business.

She's usually right, to be fair, but the woman they're taking from the cell across from ours isn't blue-dress Emma, being pulled away for a tryst with *her* guard, and I find myself watching in concern as the woman in question tries to fight the two guards off. My hands clench to fists in the dirty blanket, but I can do nothing but watch as one of them gets tired of the struggle and hits her over the back of the head with his baton.

She crumples, and they carry her limp body away.

Nausea hits me, hard and fast. I stumble out of my bed as quietly as possible, and heave up the little bit of water in my stomach into the small sink.

But the nausea lingers, just like the replays of violence behind my eyes.

Even if we escape this hell, I'm not sure I'll ever get the pieces of me back that this place has chipped away.

CHAPTER NINETEEN

RECOVERY BITES

DEMY

I wake hungry and angry the next morning, my rage at a low simmer that I just can't stifle, no matter how hard I try. Fresh air and sunshine revived that spark inside of me, and I'm finding those embers harder to tamp out a second time.

I suppose I should be grateful that my anxiety has stayed as quiet as it has, but this morning I don't have any room inside my body for gratefulness. I'm full to bubbling already, and if I'm not careful, it's going to overflow.

"You feeling okay? They didn't start you on the shots, did they?" Sherese asks.

So much for puking quietly last night.

"Shots?" I ask, deciding to skip acknowledgement of my late-night illness.

She hums a sound low in her throat, washing her hands meticulously, and cleaning underneath each fingernail before moving on to smoothing down her eyebrows and straightening her braids. "The woman they took last night for surgery. She'd have been getting daily shots for a few weeks, now. Once the shots start, you know the surgery is a matter of time."

"They took her for surgery? It looked like they were just . . ."

Killing her. It looked like they were dragging her out to kill her, but I couldn't utter the words.

"The guards will take any excuse to be rough. *Most* of them." She sniffed haughtily, arranging a small hand towel next to our dented stainless sink bowl. "But she was too new to be culled out, except for surgery."

The word "culled" sends a bucket of ice water surging through my veins, but I do my best to focus on the point.

"What's the surgery for?"

Sherese shrugs. "None of us know, and nobody will say, not even Manuel. But you come back with laparoscopic incisions on your abdomen."

Her own hand flutters down, a slight frown and a crease between her eyebrows tell me that she's already experienced it.

"So that's it—they start shots, and then it's just a game of roulette?"

"No, they will withhold your food for a full day, right before."

I nod, feeling relieved to have a tiny bit more information. The withholding food makes sense, probably because they have to put you under. Although they're not shy about withholding food for any reason, at least there's some predictability to it.

Manuel comes to let us out of our cell, and we follow idly behind him as he lets the rest of the women out into the cramped, short hallway. It's chaos, since there's no divider anymore, but I find Nell easily enough.

The massive new shiner she's sporting causes a fresh wave of fury which nearly drags me under.

"What the heck happened to you? You were fine when they put me in my cell," I whisper close to her ear, where we can't be overheard in the general racket of nearly fifty women plus the guards in one confined space.

"I got a visit a few hours later. The nurse, with two guards. They went to a couple of cells, and some of the girls got shots. Someone in my cell did—she has so many marks on the backs of her arms—and then they grabbed me, too."

A chill runs down my spine, but I keep my mouth shut as my brain freewheels through the information Sherese shared this morning.

Do I tell her? Will it *matter*, or just make things worse for her?

There is already dread all over her face, and I can't bring myself to add to it. I will tell her soon. Before they can progress to surgery.

Besides, unless they move to daily shots, it could be anything.

It could be anything, but it's not.

The ominous little voice at the back of my head won't shut up, and as I eat my tray of slop, my gaze keeps wandering back to her arm, and the big, ugly, fingerprint-shaped bruises below the injection point.

I've got to get us out of here before they can do permanent harm.

CHAPTER TWENTY

PLUMB AND PONDER

FLETCHER

Atlas's pacing is going to drive me berserk. But it helps him think, and at this point, we need a fresh idea. We're still camped in a mobile command center near the bunker, while what seems like a hundred NAA analysts scour every inch of it.

But every minute that passes, the feeling that they're further in the wind grows, and now, twenty-four hours later, the hope we had has waned into untenable frustration. I run a frustrated hand through my hair, disrupting my bun for the tenth time in two hours. I snatch the elastic out, and consider shooting it across the room.

Begrudgingly, I twist my hair back up and out of my face with it instead.

"There's got to be a clue. You don't move *that* many people without leaving some trace. You just *don't*," Glitch mutters under his breath, idly swiping his tablet. He's hunched over a long conference table, and nothing but his eyes and his fingers have moved in the two hours we've been locked into this room.

"There are traces, we just don't know what they are. The external cameras were all disabled when they started to evacuate." Atlas's words are flat, just a shade above dead.

If I hadn't seen him nearly bring down a porch roof with anger, I'd think he didn't care his wife was gone. Instead, I recognize it for what it is. A mask, a shield.

I want to shake him until the angry man comes back, the one who *did stuff*, even if it was destructive. I'd like to punch a four-by-four myself right now. *Something. We've got to do something before they take her further away.*

"Okay, so, let's stop trying to look for what they did. Put yourself in their shoes. You've got a couple hundred people to move, a chunk of them prisoners. How do you do it in broad daylight, without tripping any of our protocols? Where are the gaps?" Glitch asks, straightening in his chair.

"Trucks, obviously, from the tire tracks."

Glitch sighs. "Trucks need roads. But that's the last gimme. How would *you* do it? Ignore the evidence. Ignore everything we know. You're here, and you've got to escape. Give me something."

"Box trucks," I say, mind spinning. "Delivery vehicles. Things wrapped to look like legitimate businesses, but aren't."

"Stolen?" Glitch asks, flicking his gaze between me and Atlas, as if weighing the other man's reactions.

"No, not stolen," Atlas supplies, pausing his pacing. "Legitimately purchased, but the *lettering* stolen."

Glitch starts typing. "Give me more. Don't forget that Nell and Demy are among the prisoners. If you were them, how would you get a signal to us? A message."

Atlas rubs a hand over his weary face, sighing. "Anything, Glitch. Nell knows my line of work. It could be a sharpie note left on a park bench. It could be her wedding ring in a stranger's mailbox. Shoot, it could be an emergency repair call. Had one of those a month before we left for the NLC."

"A park bench, really?" I ask, amused by the idea of something so mundane leading to anything important.

"Really. We worked a case where we were tasked to find a kidnapping victim before the ransom time was up. We knew what block the signals were coming from, but canvasing is slow work, and it was a densely populated area. An electrician was called in for a shorted-out panel, saw a padlock inside the house, and reported it to our men at the perimeter. The girl was in the basement." He resumes pacing.

"You're not going to believe this . . ." Glitch trails off, fingers flying over his tablet. There was a plumbing call this morning about four hours northeast of here. "Toilet failure, broken internal component that caused it to overflow. But the weird thing is, the plumber found a three-carat ruby earring inside the tank."

"A ruby earring?" Atlas turns to Glitch. "Is there a photo? I don't think Nell had any rubies. It's weird, but might be related."

"Yeah, here." He spins the tablet and lifts it, so both of us can see it. I'm on my feet in a second.

"That's Demy's earring, I'm ninety-nine percent sure of it. We'd need to ask Beckett because he gave her the gaudy getup as a courting gift. But it matches the heels that carved her legs all up."

"*What*, now? How can shoes carve up your legs?"

"Real gems and settings are sharp, and they don't belong on straps tied to your legs." I had to bite back my irritation at the memory of her being wounded because of a dang pair of shoes. *Some gift.*

She and I agreed that the best gift was the exercise gear we both loved so much. When I get her back, I'm going to take her to one of the fancy sporting goods stores and let her buy the whole place. Anything she wants, anything to put a smile on her face after going through this hell.

Atlas was already dialing, and a second later Beckett was on a video feed. "Beckett, is this one of the earrings you gave Demy as a courting gift?" He points the tablet at Glitch's, and Beckett is quiet for a long moment.

"Yes, that is one of the pair I gave Demelza."

Atlas hangs up on Beckett, not bothering to discuss it further. "We've got a direction, let's roll out—but just our immediate group. If it's close, I don't want to spook them."

The way station is *too* nice to be so rural. It's incongruous even to me, who knows nothing about city planning. Glitch is already in a back room, hooking up to the place's security feed, over the protests of a very nervous-looking manager. Atlas and I, on the other hand, are barging into the ladies' bathroom. It's a single stall and thankfully empty, so I lock the door behind us.

He doesn't waste time, going straight to the toilet and lifting off the back. I don't see anything out of the ordinary, though I've admittedly not spent much time looking in toilet tanks.

He frowns, then pushes the plunger to flush it and drain the water. The inside pieces all look brand new, which makes sense.

"There," he breathes, crouching down and pointing at the back, right below the water line.

I lean in closer, and sure enough, there's something scratched very faintly into the wall of the tank.

Underground.

That's it. No other message, besides a small arrow, pointing due east.

"She was here. Nell would be the only person who'd know I could clue off a toilet." Atlas stands, replacing the lid, and running a hand through his hair, stopping to fist the ends. He's so tense, a lesser man would snap under the force of it.

I know because I feel ready to snap, too. I'm walking around on a hair trigger, and it has to be just as bad for him.

But the earring is Demy's, which means that sometime in the last twenty-four hours, she was standing in this very room.

We're close. And for the second time since they were taken, we have a solid direction.

I'm coming for you, Demy. Hang on for me.

CHAPTER TWENTY-ONE

DESPERATION

DEMY

T hings have settled back into the same old routine by evening. When we're picked up for dinner, the line is more orderly, as well as more subdued. We've been well broken, brought to heel once more. The fury still simmers, though. Still bubbles behind my breastbone like I'm set to combust on a short fuse.

Nell hasn't acquired any more bruises since I last saw her, which helps a bit. I go to get into the line for a tray, but Sherese shakes her head, and pulls me along to a table with no food.

"Sherese, Lee hasn't brought me any food yet," I attempt to argue, but she's got a death grip on my arm.

"He won't if you keep getting in the line. You have to be open to receive." She sits, chin held high, and pats the bench at her side. I slide into it with a sigh but adopt a similar pose to hers. She's been right so far, and I suppose it would be nice to stop eating mystery meat.

Nell arches a brow at me from across the room but keeps any knowing smirks to herself. We haven't actually *discussed* this—me having a jail-boyfriend—but I hope she knows that I'm doing this for a reason.

To my surprise, it's less than two minutes before Manuel walks in our direction with a tray for Sherese, and hot on his heels is Lee, with a tray for me. The third guard peels away with a tray for Emma. Manuel smiles widely at Sherese, slipping the tray in front of her, but I can't focus on their interaction, because Lee is sliding a tray in front of me, too.

"We don't have many choices, but I hope you like plums," he murmurs, smiling proudly as he gestures to his offering.

I nod, forcing a pleasant expression. "I've never had one before," I admit.

He scoffs, adjusting the collar of his cloak before leaning in, invading my personal space. I can feel his breath on my cheek when he speaks. "I'm sure you'll like it. They're *juicy* when you bite into them." The look he levels on me has me freezing, discomfort pooling in my hands and feet and manifesting as sweaty palms as his arm comes around my back.

I'm stiff—I know he's going to notice—but he doesn't seem to care as he grips my hand too tightly in his, tugging me into an awkward side hug.

"Loosen up, baby. It's only going to get better from here." He nips my ear, and revulsion sends bile up the back of my throat, scalding me from the inside out.

I'm going to be sick, right here on this plate he just brought me.

Hold it down, Demy. Hold it down. You can do this. You have to do this. You've survived worse. Think of the alleys you've slept in, the years you spent barely surviving the cold and damp, the filthy bathrooms you hid in. My mind goes back to that more palatable torture, disconnecting from the moment, from the feel of his hot palm rubbing over my cold flesh.

When Nell slams her tray down across from me at the table, Lee reluctantly pulls back. His hand slithers from the inside of my wrist up, up, up my arm and then painfully slowly across my back.

"I'll leave you to it," he murmurs against the shell of my ear, trying to be sultry. But I can barely hold back a shiver of disgust until he's got his back turned to me.

"You're going to have to do better, Demy, or he'll turn his attentions to someone who *welcomes* them," Sherese scolds me, and even though I want to argue, to defend myself, I still can't. I'm rooted to the seat, like if I move, make any single noise, he'll come back and keep touching me.

It's only a matter of time until he wants more, and I absolutely cannot give it to him. I'll die first, by my own hand, before I give up more than I already have.

Nell picks up my fork, and presses it into my hand, before reaching across and briskly rubbing the back of my arm. It's almost like she's working to erase him from me, the lingering *ick* from my skin.

She breaks through the shell, and a full-body shudder wracks me. I don't know what it is, only that I can't stop the shaking for nearly a minute.

"That's it, let it out. You're okay. You're *okay*," Nell soothes, and slowly, I start to believe it.

Shame flushes my face, as I finally look up from the tray, the dark, shiny plum taunting me. Its perfect purple skin is suddenly revolting, and I can't bear to look at it.

I meet Nell's eyes instead, expecting reproach. But all I see is understanding, and the first little piece of tension loosens in my chest. She knows.

"Try to eat. You need to keep your strength up. Then we can go walk," she offers, pointing at the open, basically empty holding room.

It's not rowing, but it's something. I lift my fork and eat, though I don't taste any of it—even the plum, which I roughly pull in half and share with Nell. The destruction of his little prize in the only way I'm allowed is all the satisfaction I scrape from the meal, and I take a savage glee from the purple stains on my fingers.

There is no exercise equipment at this bunker, which does *not* help. And after we finish our crappy meals in companionable silence, there's no beautiful burn of muscles to distract me from how much I hate everything about this place and all the cult-brainwashed bastards in it keeping me here. But Nell takes me by the arm and drags me to the far wall, and then we walk, making sure to keep clear of the guards. It's a slow, steady pace, and eventually she starts talking to me.

They are little, trivial stories about random things that she learned in med school. Antics she's pulled on Atlas over the years. But somewhere around the third lap, my muscles are actually loose again; the rest of the shame and numbness having been left behind on the cold concrete under my tennis shoes.

"I need to tell you something, and it's not good," I say.

"Well, with an intro like that, I can't wait to hear," Nell says lightly, though there's an undercurrent of tension to her tone.

"The daily shots mean they're going to do a surgery."

She half-pauses, leaving her step hitched, before she recovers and resumes walking. "Do you know what it's for?" Nell asks.

"No, I don't. Sherese doesn't either. Only that it's laparoscopic, and that they'll withhold your food the day before."

117

She blows out a shaky breath, and then another. "I can't let them do that, Demy. I told you, we were ready to try for kids. The shots are bad enough, but if they're doing surgery . . . they might be sterilizing people. It's the only thing that's logical."

I think about that for a while. "That would make sense, since they're not killing women, like we thought."

"They probably will eventually, but for now they seem to get a sick satisfaction from toying with us," she says bitterly.

I can't disagree. They get a lot of satisfaction from manhandling and beating us. More than half of the women wear fresh bruises, and the other half look so beaten down, they may as well be black and blue.

She looks distressed as she continues, "But what can we do? The daily injections . . . every time they stick me, I feel one step closer to losing hope. I really thought our guys would have found us, by now. But I also hadn't expected to be underground, in such a rural area. We weren't searching underground before. But my message . . . what if the toilet didn't overflow, like I thought? Or what if it did, and they missed the message?" A red flush of panic is burning up her neck; her shoulders are hunched down, and I can see her breaths coming far more rapidly than our walking pace should trigger. She's panicking at the thought, a feeling I know far too well.

I grip her fingers in mine, her bones fine, like a bird. She's hardly imposing, except she carries so much fire inside her. "Hey, don't go down that path. It's not helpful, and we have no way of knowing. We are going to keep working towards getting ourselves out of here, and if they show up before then, the more help the merrier. Right?"

"Right," she says, but there's no conviction. The squeeze she gives my fingers in return is half-hearted, at best. Her mind has gone on to another place, the most terrifying one she knows. I understand it, even if it doesn't help.

"So, we need to step things up a notch," I say, thinking aloud. Maybe I can distract her with a plan. It's not much, but it's what I used to do when I was younger, living in rat-infested alleys, and hiding in electric train bathrooms. I'd lock myself down, not move a muscle. But I'd plan. And re-plan. Un-plan, sharpen, and go again. Over and over, I'd run through every possibility, until all that was left was to move when daylight came.

"How do we do that?" Nell asks.

"I . . ." I have no idea. But I can't say that. Plus, it's not true. I have *one* idea. A very, very dangerous one. But she pulled me back from the edge, and now it's my turn. The only way we get out of this is together, and I'm not some fainting flower who's never experienced danger. "I'll ask Lee to take me back up top. See if I can leave another message, or find us a way out."

Chapter Twenty-Two

No Dice

Fletcher

"We've got nothing." Glitch lets an uncharacteristic curse fly and slams his messenger bag down on the table of our temporary headquarters. We've commandeered an office building across the rural highway from the gas station—Atlas waved a fat wad of cash under the manager's nose, and he was more than happy to pass over the keys for a week—and the break room is serving as our war room.

"The gas station denied you access to the footage?" Atlas asks, knuckles white on the back of the chair next to mine. I can't remember the last time I saw him sit down, but he doesn't seem the type to appreciate a mother hen, so I'm keeping my mouth shut. If this is his process, I want him in it.

I want Demy back, and I'm willing to do whatever it takes to get her safely away from the Cabal, even if that means letting every single one of us burn ourselves to the end of our wicks.

"Oh, no. I got access to every single scrap they have, on the current hard drive and two back-up drives. Even made the manager haul out the new one, which is unfortunately fresh from the factory, and still blank. And do you know what I found across all the drives? Blank spaces. Tiny slivers of time erased from the stream."

The chair groans under Atlas's grip, and I cast him a pointed glance. He lets go and runs a hand over the back of his neck. Frustration is in every line of his body; I know because it matches mine. It feels like everything inside me is going to explode if we don't get a break soon.

Every second that passes, they're doing awful things to her. Every minute is a minute of torture. Every hour, some new horror.

Every day, a step closer to me not getting her back.

And I have to get her back. I can't let her go without telling her I fell for her. That I love her.

It seemed too soon, before. She was still trying to decide between Beckett and me, and I didn't want to tell her prematurely. But now? Now I'd give anything to go back, lay it all on the line.

I thought I wanted one kind of girl. A jokester, someone light and fluffy to buoy me up, make me laugh. But the more time I spent with Demy, the more I realized that her strength, her fire . . . that was what I craved. Nights laying under the stars, sharing the hard things.

She *got me* in a way that I didn't know I needed, and I should have told her.

But there's no going back, and I can't waste time wishing.

"So they've deleted their footage more than once. I assume one of the missing spots is three days ago, just before we busted the bunker?" I ask, forcing myself to focus on the here and now, instead of wallowing in what should have been.

"Yes, of course. They *were* thorough. I didn't realize any footage was missing at first, since they didn't use an electromagnet or a scrambler. It's only a twenty-minute time gap, so small that *probably* nobody would notice if they weren't looking with a fine-toothed comb. Long enough to cover a stop with an in-side-the-store visit. But they deleted every single angle of interior and exterior footage, so not only do we not get visual confirmation that Nell and Demy came to that bathroom, but we can't get a peek at what vehicle they were using. I was hoping to contact whichever company they were pretending to be, and get a list of all their valid license plates to hand off to the police." Glitch sinks down into the chair, despair dragging his shoulders down. "I'm sorry, guys. I feel like I've failed you."

Atlas freezes, the sudden absence of motion drawing my attention, and then a grin spreads over his face, a grin so ferocious, it's a little bit terrifying even though we're on the same side.

"You didn't fail, Glitch. I know exactly what we need to do." He's out of the room so quickly I nearly knock my chair over trying to catch him, because there's no chance I'm missing whatever this breakthrough is. I dog his steps as he bolts out of the building and across the empty highway toward the gas station.

"Want to share with the class?" I huff as I slow to a jog now that I've caught him.

"They've deleted the footage more than once, presumably every time the Cabal uses this way station. Look at this place." He waves a hand as we step back into the parking lot of the gas station, gesturing to the shiny white exterior and brand-spanking-new pumps with all the bells and whistles. "This is the kind of station you expect to see near the Capitol in Wrightsville, not out in the boondocks."

"Yeah, I noticed that. But maybe somebody's got more money than sense, and this was sold as an investment—it happens."

"Or the Cabal is greasing palms. And part of that arrangement is that their visits get conveniently removed from the tapes."

"I still don't see how that helps us since the footage is gone," I argue, following hot on his heels through the station's automatic sliding doors.

"You will. Where's the manager?" he bellows, startling the lone other patron of the station, and sending her scurrying out the door with a glare tossed over her shoulder for good measure, bag of chips abandoned in her wake.

A saloon-style double door flies open at the back of the store, the disgruntled manager charging out, stumbling a bit at the end of his stride when he sees Atlas in all his gleeful fury standing in the aisle.

"What do you need, sir? I believe my employees have already complied quite generously with your investigation, and unfortunately there's nothing more we can offer you." He straightens his oddly thin tie, and does his best to make eye contact, but in seconds his gaze is skittering away off to the side, anxiety plain on his pinched features.

Atlas saunters forward, resting a meaty forearm on top of a metal shelving unit full of brightly colored candies, a few flopping free with a joyous crinkle as he leans down to eye level with the manager. He lets the silence stretch a long moment before speaking in low tones. "That's just the thing, Herb. Can I call you Herb? I feel like we're friendly now, don't you?" Atlas lets his free hand drop solidly onto the man's shoulder, making him flinch. I stand off to the side, observing with my arms crossed and eyebrows raised.

"H-Herb is fine."

"Great. Herb, I don't think you *have* complied. You see, this is a very nice station you run. Really, superb. And for such a rural area . . . this exceeds expectations a little *too well*, if you catch my drift."

"I'm sorry, but I don't—" Herb splutters, his cheeks turning red under our scrutiny.

"Ahh, ah, now. We're *friends*, Herb. And friends don't lie to one another, do they, Fletch?"

"Definitely not, Atlas. Lying to your friends is a betrayal," I agree, adding a little extra depth to the last word.

"I couldn't agree more. Now, Fletcher, it struck me just a few minutes ago that a station *this nice* with such excellent security really shouldn't have so many gaps. Not unless it was being intentionally sabotaged. And frankly, Glitch doesn't feel your employee knows a bit more than he shared. So honest, that one. Churchgoers, am I right?" Atlas squeezes the man's shoulder, and he practically wilts before my eyes.

"They are rather dependable about some things, I suppose," I offer.

"Highly. The man's been married forty years and is working here nights to put his kids through college. *Devoted.*" Atlas tuts. "But you, Herb. We haven't spoken to you yet about these snafus. So why don't you tell us? How does the footage keep getting wiped?"

"Must be a glitch! Who knows, all this stuff is so technical. I'm just a simple man." He lifts his palms in a show of innocence, but sweat is accumulating along his hairline, and thin, wispy strands are starting to stick to his neck and collar.

Guilty as a lone dog in a treat factory.

"Now, Herb, I don't feel like you're being entirely honest with me, and I don't take it lightly when my *friends* aren't honest. So why

124

don't we try this . . . one more time." He tightens his grip on Herb's shoulder, and he squeaks pitifully under Atlas's oversized paw.

"Okay, look—I don't know anything, okay? They come through every week or two. Sometimes more, sometimes less. The vehicles are always different, so are the people. We can only tell we need to ditch the footage because of the creepy cape-things they wear, and they're all skinheads. Horrible taste." His upper lip curls into a disgusted sneer.

"Focus, Herb. Who told you to delete the footage?" Atlas asks, intently focused.

"The weekend manager."

"Who's that?" Atlas's patience is growing thin, and Herb cowers away from him, face paling.

"H–his name's Chris."

"And why, exactly, did you listen to Chris? Couldn't you lose your job for tampering with the security footage?" I ask, trying to sound reasonable and calm as I edge in next to Atlas to give the man some perceived backup.

"He's the owner's son! I assumed if he told me to do it, the owner wanted it done."

Atlas immediately releases his grip and straightens. "I need Chris's number, right now."

Herb rattles off a string of numbers, and Atlas is already striding towards the door when he yells at his retreating back, "Please, you can't tell him I told you! I'll lose my ten percent cut, and my job."

Atlas spins on his heel, but I cover the distance between them in a flash, beating him to the punch and grabbing Herb by the collar as my anger wins. "Your *cut*?! My girlfriend and countless other women's *lives* are on the line, and all you care about is money. Losing your *cut* is going to be the least of your worries since

125

you're going to be charged as an accomplice to mass abductions, abuse, and murder. Don't bother trying to run. The police are already here." I pause, letting him have a moment to hear the growing sounds of sirens approaching. "But hey, maybe if you tell them everything about Chris, they'll go a little easier on you, you narcissistic jackass!"

The man's face goes pale as I shove him away. Atlas is already leaving the building, and the police sirens blast outside, filling the store for a moment when he opens the door.

There's no joy in it for me, though. All I can think about is finding this *Chris*, and figuring out what he knows about the men who kidnapped Demy. This was the break we needed.

It has to be.

CHAPTER TWENTY-THREE

THRESHING

DEMY

The evening meal is always at the same time. At what I'm guessing is a week—ten days?—into our captivity, my body has developed a new internal rhythm. So while I have no access to a clock here, my body still knows it's too early when our cell door scratches open against the concrete. Sherese hides her concern behind a placid façade, and I do my best to mirror it.

But when I sit up from my cot and see that Lee is here, holding a purple dress, with a look in his cold, dead eyes that makes me feel ill, I almost lose it. *Almost.*

"Lee?" I ask, unable to keep all of the flustered nerves out of my voice.

A smile splits his face—that feral grin that makes me want to run to Grandma's house to avoid the big, bad wolf.

Or better yet, pick up my favorite bow and shiny, sharp arrows from Peter's class, and sink one into each of those hands that he's touched me with.

"I brought you a little something," he says, his voice low and chilling, even though we're alone, besides Sherese. Although as

127

soon as she realized it was Lee, she turned to studious avoidance, arranging herself back on her cot with her back to me, facing the wall in silence.

"A dress. It's a lovely color." I force out the words, hoping he takes my nerves as excitement, and not sheer, crippling anxiety.

As he draws closer I hurriedly stand, nearly tripping as anxiety tries to lock down my muscles, but a deeper sense of self-preservation forces me to get *off* the cot. I can't be a sitting duck when he's got that predatory stride eating the ground between us. Slowly. Stalking.

"I had a feeling purple would look good on you. Like my own, shiny amethyst. Or a geode. You know about those?"

I draw a blank for a second, but then an elementary science lesson flashes in my memory, images of an ugly rock busted open to show shiny, shimmery gems inside. I nod, once I realize he's waiting for a response.

He stops inches from me, the stretchy, garish purple dress on outstretched palms, waiting. I reach out with icy fingers and take it, forcing a small smile onto my lips.

"Thank you. It will be nice to have a change of clothes so I can wash them."

He tsks. "Oh, I don't mind these. They do show off your curves." His eyes skate down my frame, leaving a trail of imaginary sludge on my body in their wake.

It might be imaginary, but I'll sure as heck try to scrub the feel of it off once he's safely gone and I'm alone.

"But there's just something so *delightful* about a dress." He doesn't elaborate, but he does reach up and skim his fingers across my collar bones, safely hidden behind my exercise top for now.

I swallow hard and look down at my feet. "I'm sure it's lovely, thank you."

I hate myself for the words, but Nell's terror at being sterilized in some dangerous, unknown surgery is forefront in my mind. I've done worse than lie to survive. I've stolen, I've trespassed. I've fought tooth and nail to survive, and now that I've got someone to protect there might not be a limit to what I'll do, even if I hate *every second* of it.

"You're welcome. I can't wait to see you wearing it." He lets his hands wander up, touching a loose lock of hair, which escaped from my braid while I was lying down. I have to lock down every muscle in my body to stop the shiver of revulsion that desperately wants to roll through me. He's going to keep expecting—*taking*—more and more, and the thought makes me want to sob and scream at the same time. I've got to think fast, to get things going where I need them to, and away from him pushing this further than I want it to go.

His hands have already traveled down to my neck, dancing around the edges of my ear and sending my heart hammering in fear.

"It seems a shame to waste such a beautiful gift on just going back to the holding area."

"Oh yeah?" He seems distracted, the words a bare murmur as he stares too hard at my throat.

"Yeah, it's so ugly in there. The forest you walked us through was pretty. Maybe I could wear this dress for you, and you could take me up there," I say, trying to sound casual, even hopeful.

His gaze sharpens, his eyes narrowing as he meets mine again. And then between heartbeats, his hand that was grazing my flesh wraps around my throat, squeezing—squeezing the air right out of my lungs.

Panic overwhelms me, icy-cold and surging through my veins, as I claw at his grip. But he may as well be a Titan of legend, and me a puny human who can't make fire. My nails are useless, and I can't scream—no matter how hard I try, nothing makes it past his grip besides muted, panicked squeaks.

"You're just trying to use me as a vehicle to escape, you stupid little girl. How dumb do you think I am? Huh?" He shakes me, as if further angered that I don't answer—but I *can't*. My fingers are starting to prickle, pins and needles as my oxygen runs out, and they go numb. I fight harder, kicking him in the shins, trying to knee him in the balls, but he's holding me too close to get any momentum to hurt him, and my legs are going numb, too.

"You're smokin' hot, but clearly aren't the sharpest knife in the drawer, if you think I'm just going to cart you to the surface so you can try to *run*."

Tears well in my eyes as things start to dim around the edges. I'm going to pass out, and there's nothing I can do.

I reach up again, towards his face. He might knock me out, but I'll scratch his eyes out first. The motion is too slow, though, like I'm fighting through water, or sand. I push, but my muscles aren't responding like they should, and my arm flutters weakly against his cheek before he bats it away and backs me against the wall.

God, what is he going to do to me if I pass out?

Even the sheer terror of that thought can't stop the encroaching blackness or damn up the hot spill of tears over my cheeks.

The last thing I see are his eyes widening, as if in surprise.

And then the blackness closes over me, and nothing matters anymore.

CHAPTER TWENTY-FOUR

WHEAT AND CHAFF

DEMY

When I come to, I'm lying in an unfamiliar room, on a hard, padded surface. For a split second, I'm confused. It's not my apartment that I shared with three roommates back in Missiana. It's also not my beautiful, luxury dorm room at the NLC. And then everything hits me; the kidnapping, the Cabal, and getting choked by Lee. I'm not on the floor, or my cot. I try to shove myself upward, but a new spike of terror-fueled adrenaline surges when I realize that I'm *strapped* to the table.

A broken scream escapes my lips, and then a woman's face appears above mine.

"Shhh, don't fight—don't fight. Hey, you were thrashing and I was afraid you'd fall off the exam table. I'll unstrap you, but you have to be completely calm first." It's Annie, the nurse down here. A panicked glance around the room shows we're in the medical center, and it's completely empty, save her and me.

As suddenly as it came, all the fight goes out of me, and exhaustion nearly drags me back under. I'm a limp spaghetti noodle, splatted against the wall and helpless to change a thing about my situation.

"I know, honey, I know. You're pretty banged up, but as far as I can tell you're going to be okay. Here's some cool water, it'll ease that sore throat."

As soon as she mentions it, the ache in my throat is a throbbing burn. Annie loosens the strap over my chest, and slowly lifts the head of the exam table, so that I can drink the water she hands me. "Take it slow. You're going to be sore for a while, if the nasty bruises on your neck are any indication."

I take a small sip with trembling fingers, and it both hurts and soothes at the same time. So, I take another, and another, until the cup is empty.

She takes it, crossing the room to the sink to refill it.

"Do you want to talk about it?" Annie asks, setting the cup on a tray that usually holds medical tools, but for now is blessedly clear and in reach.

My fingers latch onto a blanket and pull it all the way to my neck, barely resisting the urge to screw my eyes shut like a child and pretend I'm invisible.

God, I wish I was invisible.

"Did he—" The words hurt like hell, but I need to know, so I push through. "Did he do anything else to me?"

Annie's eyes go shuttered, and she turns towards the little station of medical supplies between my table and the one over.

"Not that I can tell without your permission, or without causing more harm. Your clothing was intact when he carried you in here."

My eyes close again, this time in relief as I take stock of the rest of my body slowly. Nothing else hurts, except—weirdly—my fingertips. I'm still wearing my stinking, dirty exercise clothes. I want to weep, but with joy or sadness, I couldn't tell you.

When Annie faces me again, her professional mask is back in place, all signs of the concern and human compassion she wore when I woke up tidily tucked away.

A whoosh of air signals the door being shoved open, and I flinch back against the exam table when Lee storms into the room.

"You were supposed to alert me as soon as she woke up," he snaps at the nurse, unholy fury rolling off the man like poisoned gas.

She raises both hands defensively. "She's been awake for less than five minutes. I've offered her water and asked two basic questions to attempt to ascertain her mental competency after her ordeal. Once I finished my exam, I *would* have come to get you. I can't leave her unattended if she's got a problem that needs to be dealt with."

Lee waves her off and crosses the room to my bedside. I flinch back. It's automatic, and I can't stop it.

He doesn't stop, crowding forward into my personal space, brushing my hair back away from my face as if he's a concerned lover, and not the man who did this to me.

"Shhh, it's okay, Demy, I'm here now. I'm sorry I wasn't with you when you woke up; I was on rotation."

Shock or numbness hold my tongue paralyzed, and I just stare in mute terror while he acts like *he didn't do this.* I cast a panicked gaze at Annie, but she's shuffled off to her desk, against the far wall, and is pointedly ignoring this exchange.

Doesn't she know? How can she just *leave me like this* if she knows he's the one who hurt me?

"Look at me, I want to see you," he demands, grabbing hold of my chin and pulling my face toward his, instead of Annie's back. His eyes are a little less cold and dead than usual, and I'm not sure if that's more or less alarming. "There are those beautiful brown eyes," he murmurs, running his thumb over my chin, as if I'm a scared animal, and not a woman he just brutalized.

Fury starts to build, pushing the numbness back, bringing life back to my limbs. I reach up and shove his hand off of me.

His lips press into a flat, angry line, but he lets me dislodge him.

"You did this to me—you don't get to touch me." I sound hoarse, but there's fire behind the words nonetheless, and I'm proud of it. Is it wise?

No.

Do I care?

Hell no.

"Demy, be reasonable—"

"I am being reasonable! I made a *real request* to spend time with you, and instead of seeing that for what it was, you took it badly and choked me half to death! I never want to see you again, and you can take your purple dress and *stuff it*." I push weakly against his chest, but he doesn't even sway against the pitiful effort. "I would rather keep wearing these dirty, stinking clothes until they are rags than *ever* accept another gift from you."

I cross my arms over my chest and stare him down. I might sound like a pack-a-day-smoker after a chest cold, but I am dead serious. I will find us another way out of here.

Crap.

Nell.

The rest of it comes rushing back in a stomach-dropping flood, and I close my eyes against the tears that threaten to drown me.

No, no, no. She doesn't have time for me to start over. She is getting shots every day, which means there's a surgery to sterilize her looming over her shoulder, and I can't let that happen. She's strong, but the loss of a dream like that? I can't be responsible for that happening to her, if there's *anything* I can do about it, no matter how distasteful it is.

No matter how bad it hurts.

"Hey, now, look—I'm sorry, okay? You're right. I overreacted. The truth is, I've . . . I've had a girlfriend before. It didn't end well. She used me to get closer to another guard, and I just—snapped." I let my eyes drift open and see him rubbing a hand over his shaved head.

There's ash-blonde stubble there, and on closer look, I realize he really is out of sorts about this. It doesn't excuse it—not by a million miles—but maybe this is the break I needed, no matter how awful, to get us out of this hellhole.

What I say next matters, and I have to choose my words very carefully. It burns me to my very soul, but the image of Nell, shoulders hunched and tears tracking down her face at the idea of not being able to have a child with Atlas is front and center in my mind. So, I push down the revulsion, and the hatred, and all the negative emotions I feel for this man, and I say the one thing that opens the door back for him, the words like acid as they drip from my lips.

"Am I your girlfriend?"

Hope, fervent and zealous, blooms in his dead eyes. The sight of it chills me to the bone. "If you'll still have me."

I let the silence stretch, looking down at my hands, fidgeting with my blanket, anywhere but his eyes. Anywhere but at the sick hope that turns my stomach. I put it there, and a sick little part of me asks if I'm any better than him—leading him on—but I shove it down. I'm surviving, and I won't apologize for it.

He leans in close to my ear, that thing he so loves to do, and whispers, his hot breath brushing my neck, "I'll take you to the surface if you'll give me another chance. Wear my dress."

The words send a frisson of dark hope through me, so sharp it flays open my ribcage. Tears spring to my eyes yet again, and I nod, silently. Just once.

But it's enough. He pulls back, and lets his fingers linger on the base of my neck for a second before turning to Annie.

"I've got to get back to my shift. I'll come pick her up after and return her to her cell. See that she eats something," he says, all cold indifference, as if I'm his prize hunting dog, not a grown woman with her own thoughts and desires.

"Yes, sir," she murmurs, watching him leave, judgment hooding her eyes. Annie stays at her desk and, other than serving me a bowl of soup that someone brings an hour or so later, she doesn't speak with me or look at me again.

Chapter Twenty-Five

SKIRTING THE LINE

Demy

Lee remains true to his word, and something's shifted inside him since *the incident.* That's what I call it, in my head. I can't think about it any harder than that, or I'm back to wanting to claw the man's eyes out, not play nice and pretend.

After three days of wearing his dress, day in, day out, my sink-scrubbed personal clothes are starting to taunt me from where I folded and stored them under the foot of my cot—Sherese's idea.

We walk in our single-file line to breakfast, where I sit down next to Sherese at a different table from Emma. Nell waits in line, shooting nervous glances at me every four seconds while she inches along toward her tray.

Lee and Manuel bring our breakfast of chicken, beans, and a star-shaped fruit I've never tried before. To my surprise, on my tray, and mine alone, there's half of a blueberry muffin. It's crusted with sugar, and I can smell the sweet, fruity scent of it before I even pick it up.

Lee leans down, his hand hot where it brushes over my thigh in the thin, stretchy material of the dress. Nausea roils in my stomach at the suggestive touch, but I pretend I'm a statue, waiting for whatever whispered message he sees fit to bestow on me today.

"Tonight's the night. I hope you're ready." He squeezes my thigh—*far* too close to my hip for comfort—and then walks away.

Tears gather along my eyelids as I blankly stare at the muffin.

"You must have really pleased that man," Sherese observes, tone frosty as she picks up her star fruit and takes a delicate bite.

"I— I—" The words won't come out.

Nell slams her palms down on the table across from me.

"There is something *wrong* with that woman! I swear, she gets joy by feeding off others' misery!"

Sherese arches a dark eyebrow at the outburst.

"Who?" I ask, clinging onto anything that gets my head out of the ugly thoughts I was just swimming in.

"Erin! The one who attacked you and who is currently cozying up to Emma." She waves angrily over her shoulder, where sure enough the aggressive redhead is sitting right next to Emma, looking prim in her blue dress.

"What did she do now?" Sherese prods, curious now that her nemesis is involved.

"Lara was crying in line because Erin shoved her down. But instead of caring about anyone besides herself, she's over there bragging about how she's sleeping with a guard, and she's going to be the next one to get a dress."

I shrug, not really caring who else gets what, so long as we get out of here.

Come on, Atlas . . . and maybe Beckett and Fletcher. Are they looking for me with the same fervency with which Atlas is searching for Nell?

I'd give anything for a way out, at this point. My thigh feels like it has a handprint branded on it, and if I think about what it means, what he thinks is coming . . . I suck in a too-shallow breath, and then another, unable to stop myself from succumbing to the panic.

"Demy, did you hear me? Demy!" Nell reaches across the table and shakes my bare shoulder.

I meet her eyes and shake my head.

"She's claiming she's getting a *purple* dress. *From Lee.*"

My thoughts spin, not latching onto what she's implying for a long few seconds.

Oh. *Oh.*

"Erin's sleeping with Lee?"

"That's what she'd like everyone to believe, but who knows if it's true." Nell purses her lips, shooting a distasteful look over her shoulder at the woman in question.

"Okay," I mumble, not really caring.

"Okay? What's going on with you?" Nell drops her voice, leaning forward. "You look pale. Did something happen?"

I keep my eyes fixed on my plate, and I know the moment hers find the muffin, because she gasps. "Uh, what does *that* mean?"

"It means he's sharing his personal rations with her," Sherese answers, still calmly eating her own meal. "And it's crass to sit around speculating what *else* it may mean."

I look up and catch Sherese glancing quickly away from my neck. My ugly bruise necklace is starting to turn green around the edges, and she's neither asked what happened, nor if I'm okay. She was lying right there, close enough to have helped—but she didn't. That fact has soured what there was of our friendship, though we still share a room and a place at the meal table. Although, something else dawns on me in the same second.

Nell has no tray. They're withholding her food, which means—

Sick realization twists my stomach.

For the first time since we've been here, I can't bring myself to eat. My breaths are still wrong, and after a precursory check of the guards on duty, I shove my tray across to Nell. "Take it. I'm not hungry this morning."

I swing my legs around carefully—I'm not giving any of these creeps a show, and my dress isn't floor length, like the other two—and climb off the bench. I walk myself to the farthest corner of the room, and sink down to the ground, curling into the cold wall, my back to the room.

The soft whisper of Nell's feet on concrete is my only warning before she's there, wrapping me up in her arms.

"Nell, you need to go eat," I insist, weakly shoving at one of her arms.

"Hush," she scolds me, not budging. "If they're doing a surgery tomorrow, me eating won't stop it. It will add risk, and I doubt they have the kind of equipment needed here to handle any complications. So no, I don't need to eat."

She pulls me to the side and tucks my head under her chin, much like my mom used to do when I was little. Comforting me, even when her own worst nightmare is looming.

"Tell me, or don't. But I'm here. You're not alone, no matter how it feels. I wish—" Her voice cracks, but she clears her throat and soldiers on. "I wish I could do more, but at the very least, I'm here."

I let her hold me, following her slow, deep breathing until my own returns to normal.

"Tonight is the night. We're going to the surface," I whisper. I'm determined, even as the sickness threatens to overwhelm me and make me dry heave.

She stiffens against me, the import of that statement heavy. She knows what the lack of tray for her means, but she hasn't even mentioned it. She won't ask. Not even for herself, for her *dream*.

"Do not have sex with that man, thinking it's going to get us out of here. Do you hear me? Not for me, not for anyone." She shakes my shoulders lightly, looking deeply into my eyes, an aching sadness in hers. "I mean it, Demy. Use your head, take any chance you get to leave a message. But . . . it's personal. It's *personal*, and I think you'll regret it, if you let it go that far. And Lee, the way he looks at you . . . the deeper you get, the closer he's going to watch us. That man creeps me all the way out, and I already don't like how possessive he is of you."

Is she right? Am I tightening a noose around my own neck by playing this game?

The thought is disturbing, but I shove it aside. We work with what we have, and we deal with the consequences. Those are the rules of survival, and I'm not going to apologize if the first strategy doesn't work out.

"I won't let it go that far." I shudder. "But I have to try. There's got to be a way for us to get out of here. *Tonight*, before it's too late."

"There is. There's always a way, we just have to find it," she agrees, squeezing me tightly, just as the women start lining up to head back to the cells.

Dinner comes and goes, still with no food for Nell. The lights are set to the dimmer night cycle, and Sherese is snoring softly when Lee comes for me. The soft scrape of the door over the concrete floor sends goosebumps up my arms and across my chest, but I force myself to keep breathing normally.

I've put in an effort, finger-combing and braiding my hair, washing my face, and wearing his dress. I hope he'll perceive me as eager to spend time with him, and if I'm less than receptive to his physical advances, he'll take it as nerves. Because I *am* nervous.

For all I promised Nell I wouldn't let him take things too far, he's already shown he's willing to use physical violence if I upset him. I'm not so naïve as to believe that wouldn't be true in other situations, too. I don't have any weapons but my own skill, so I'm going to stay alert and redirect him as much as possible.

Did I also put on my stretchy exercise pants underneath this dress as an extra barrier? Dang right I did.

I can do this.

I *have to do this.*

I stand from my cot and cross the distance between us, offering my hand. Lee takes it, his skin cold against mine and a crooked smile on his face. He's silent as he locks the cell door from the outside, and as he leads me through the tunnels to the surface exit. I'm surprised that we don't see another soul, not on guard or even just meandering the halls, and I can't help but wonder if there is a curfew he's breaking, or if he pulled strings to get us a window.

Either way, the exterior door is solid steel, and it takes some effort for him to crack it open. When the cool night air hits my face, I suck in a deep, grateful lungful.

The door settles back into place behind us, and I look around at our surroundings. We're lucky that there's a waxing moon to light the ground between the trees, but it's eerily quiet out here. No bugs chirping or night birds rustling, and that fact reminds me that I'm with a predator, and I must stay alert.

"So, you really do like the outdoors, huh?" Lee asks as he slips an arm around my shoulders and leads me away from the bunker entrance. I do my best to spot landmarks, but honestly the trees here all look the same, so there's not much to go on.

"I do. Doesn't it make you feel more alive?"

He shrugs, seeming bored. "Outside's fine, but inside's good, too."

Such a conversationalist. He at least seems content to walk in silence, leading me further into the foliage.

"Where are we going?" I ask after a few minutes of walking in a straight line.

"Just getting a little distance. There's a night patrol and, while he's cool, if he sees us he has to send us back inside."

Good to know.

"Oh, okay," I murmur, keeping it light. Eventually we stop, and I'm excited to see the first real landmark. It's a gnarled and twisted tree, bent from some past storm so it touched the ground before it continued growing upward, forming a natural bench about five feet across. The bark is worn smoother in some spots, meaning this is a popular spot to sit. He sits first, and I choose a spot a reasonable distance away and turn so I'm sitting sideways, facing him but not inviting him to touch me.

"So, how did you come to be part of the Cabal?" I ask one of the questions I prepared to keep him talking, and hopefully garner some useful information for when we're out of here.

He looks at me curiously, but doesn't seem offended by the question. "I joined when I was seventeen, right after the government took my girlfriend. A buddy of mine told me there was a group doing something about the corruption. Working to restore purity to human bloodlines."

I'm so floored by the candid response, you could knock me over with a feather.

He thinks he's helping people. Is he completely delusional? Is brainwashing part of their induction process? I realize it's been too long, so I blurt the first thing that comes to mind.

"Is that even possible? Who even knows what a 'pure' human looks like, anyways? We've all been modified by the Sterilization Vector somewhere along the line."

He snorts, shaking his head. "See, you've believed the government line. We *know* better. Purity of our bloodline is in reach, we just all have to be willing to sacrifice to get there."

There's a fervency to his words, in a way I've never heard before, and it terrifies me. This man believes every word he's saying with a dangerous level of zeal. Purity of bloodlines? That's creepy genocide stuff, and I have never wanted to both deck somebody and run away at the same time quite as badly I do right now.

"I—" I swallow hard, mind reeling for some way to respond that doesn't give away my utter revulsion, but that also keeps him talking. "I never knew. The rumors say that the Cabal just kidnaps and murders women, but you're keeping us alive . . ."

He snorts. "We let those rumors run wild. Healthy fear keeps people in line," he says, eyes going flat again. It's like he's reciting something he memorized, something he was told over and over again.

"Your organization has always had the . . . 'monster under the bed' kind of feeling. Like the boogeyman, or Krampus. And yet, here we are . . ." I pick at a piece of bark on the side of the tree we're sitting on, hoping that he hasn't picked up on my level-nine-thousand internal creep out.

"Yet here we are . . ." He lifts up my hand, tracing the back of my knuckles with his thumb. "You know, I didn't expect you to be so understanding." I can hear the suspicion in his tone, matching the tense set of his shoulders.

I shrug, letting the motion naturally pull my hand from his. "What choice have I got? There's no way out. We're always under lock and key, or surveillance. At least if I understand, that's something."

A grin stretches across his face with painstaking slowness, the look sending a chill over my skin. "I knew you were the one for me. You *get* it. You're smarter than the rest. Everyone else just squabbles and fights, trying to be queen of the trash heap. But not you." He reaches up and thumbs my cheek, and I have to fight not to pull back.

Small touches aren't dangerous. They're the price I pay for a chance. A sliver of hope.

A rustle in the trees snags his attention, and he shoots to his feet, placing a finger on his lips in a reminder for me to stay quiet.

I freeze, letting my eyes roam over the inky shadows that surround us. He takes a few steps, startling a small, skittering rodent out of its hidey-hole and sending it scurrying off deeper into the woods.

He snorts. "Just a deer mouse."

"A deer mouse? I've never heard of those before."

"They're native to New Texas," he murmurs, and I file the tidbit away with all the glee of a child finding a piece of rock candy at the back of the pantry. "Nocturnal. We probably just interrupted his nightly dinner forage."

"You're so smart," I murmur, standing up from the fallen tree as an idea sparks in my mind. "I bet you know what kind of trees these are, too." I cross the small space of forest floor, then let my hands trail around the rough bark of the closest standing tree as I circle it. "Like this one. Do you know what it is?"

"That's a pine. They're all over the southern regions, until you get too far south."

"See? I knew you'd know."

"Doesn't everybody?"

"I've never seen one of these up in the Chitucky area." I pull a tri-state out of thin air, not wanting to tell him any of the places I lived most recently, even if it's a petty detail.

"They don't do well in clay-heavy soils," Lee adds with a predatory smile, stalking around the tree-bench and caging me against the rough pine bark. He drops his mouth next to my cheek, and I try my best not to panic at the closeness; the same position he was in when he choked me.

Focus, Demy. Focus.

"Pines like acidic, free-draining soil," he whispers, as if it's some kind of love talk, and I force a laugh.

"Okay, show-off, point taken." I rest a hand on his shoulder, pushing him back a bit to give myself some breathing room. "I've got a more serious question, though."

He arches a pale-blonde eyebrow at me and waits for it.

"Do you have a knife?"

He stiffens under my fingertips, and I shake my head. "Not for anything bad. It's just . . . this is our first *real* date. I thought we should commemorate the occasion. You know, carve our initials into the tree." *Or my first name, so when people come looking, they know I was here.*

With any luck, I can sneak something directional into the carving, so people know which direction to look for the bunker.

He throws his head back and laughs, the sound chilling more than happy.

"I never know what to expect from you." He leans in and plasters a kiss to my lips before I can dodge or pull away. His lips are dry and clammy, and I resist the urge to gag under the assault. Using my hand on his shoulder, I manage to push him away after a count of ten. "You're perfect for me," he murmurs, before finally stepping back out of my personal space.

"And *of course*, I've got a knife. Standard issue." He reaches into his cloak and shows me a black weapons belt, fastened around his waist. There's a pistol, the butt of some other weapon I don't recognize, and two different knives.

He reaches for the smaller of the two and pulls out a folding multi-purpose knife about as long as my palm is wide. "Where should we put it?"

"Probably on the side facing *away* from the bench, so you don't get in trouble. Once it's scabbed over, nobody will ever know it was us." I walk to the back side of the tree, and point to a spot.

"Okay, then. Just our initials?"

"What if we do our first names?"

He snorts. "Demy, we can't plaster our names on here. I would get in trouble if I gave them proof we broke the rules and brought you up here."

Shoot. How am I going to send a message if I can't use my own name? What's another name they'd know was us?

An idea hits me.

"Let's make up code names. You know, names that nobody inside the bunker has, so they won't suspect us, even if someone finds it."

"I'll be Lance, then." He shoots me a cocky grin, and starts carving the L into the tree. I watch in silence as he finishes his name, when the crunching of pine needles stops him, C half finished.

"Shoot, that's the perimeter guard. Guess we're done out here." He folds the knife shut with a soft click, and dread fills me.

"Wait, give me the knife. You go talk to him, and I'll finish up." I hold out my palm for the knife. He hesitates for a long second, and I know it's a lot to ask. But how far will his newfound guilt carry me?

He drops the blade into my palm, then takes a couple steps towards the bench, calling out to the guard.

"Hey, Benji!"

I ignore their resulting conversation, making quick work of the name I've chosen. I just have to hope Fletcher is with the search party, or else this will all be for nothing.

The name is rough, but large, and easily spotted if you're looking. I opt for some little confetti-like dashes around the names instead of the traditional heart and manage to sneak a curved arrow in at the top. If you didn't look closely, you'd completely miss it. But I'm betting the farm on the idea that Fletcher will be looking *very* closely.

I fold the knife closed, and peek around the edge of the tree. They're still talking, and worry begins to creep up the back of my neck that Lee will send this Benji off, and then I won't have anything else to distract him with. He's already kissed me, and that's more than enough unwanted physical contact for one night. I've got to move quickly because it looks like the conversation is winding to a close. I look regretfully down at the weapon in my hand. Do I dare try to sneak it into my bra? It would be amazing to have that up my sleeve, but I don't have a way to hide it without Sherese knowing, and we're not on the best of terms.

That plan also runs the risk of him not believing me, searching, and finding it.

As quietly as I can, I drop the folding knife at the base of this tree, kicking a rock in front of it for a bit of camouflage. Better to know it's out here, and have a weapon if we manage to get back outside, than risk losing it inside.

With that settled, I make a show of tripping over another rock as loudly as I can, stumbling and catching myself on the side, in plain view of the two men.

"Oh, no," I whisper, feigning dread at spoiling our outing. I quickly step back behind the trunk, but the damage is done.

"You brought a woman out here? Are you friggin' serious? Hey, you! Get over here, now!" Benji shouts the command.

I step back out and slowly walk towards the two men, hanging my head and arrowing towards Lee's side. Benji snatches my arm, hard, and keeps it locked in his vise-like grip. *That's going to bruise.*

"This little field trip is over. *Now.*" He shoots a pointed look at Lee, who's fuming as he dogs our steps.

Benji makes quick work of dragging me to the bunker door, levering it open and pushing me through.

"Can I trust that you'll lock her back up, or do I need to leave my patrol, too, just like you did?" the man snaps.

"I've got it, Ben. It was just a harmless walk in the woods." He waves off the other man's concern, then takes my arm in the exact same spot Benji just left bruises. Rather than gently, though, he digs his nails into my already tender flesh, and can't hold back a whimper at the pain. "It won't happen again."

There's a cold promise underlying the words, and I know it's directed at me. Fear spikes my heart rate as the massive steel door clicks shut between me and freedom, leaving me alone in the pitch blackness with a violent, angry man.

CHAPTER TWENTY-SIX

WOOD SIGN

FLETCHER

Three more days have passed, and I'm going nearly out of my mind, knowing we're this close, and yet we still haven't found any sign of where they're hiding the women. Chris, the weaselly shop owner, wasted no time rolling over and giving us everything he had, as well as releasing the original footage of the women entering their building. It was enough and led us about two hours east of their fueling station.

Glitch was even thrilled to get a shot of the trucks they've been using and has BOLOs out on every one he pulled from their footage.

Meanwhile the sight of Demy, wearing the same clothes she was last seen in, dirty and banged up, walking through the glass doors with one of those bald bastards' hands on her almost sent me over the ledge.

Which is why I'm spending every single daylight hour roaming the woods, looking for something, *anything* that's a sign. Each day I get deeper and deeper, building off where I ended the day before. Glitch has drones scouring the skies, with operators watching the monitors twenty-four seven. The NAA police are speaking with every single company the trucks were labeled as for any recent thefts and lists of valid plate numbers.

But I can't just sit on my hands, waiting for someone else to drop her in my lap. If there's anything I can do, no matter how small, I'll do it.

Unlike Beckett.

I punch the nearest tree trunk as I pass it, fury at his *laissez-faire* attitude towards a woman he's supposed to love. I know I can't *stop* her from choosing him, and, sure, he also got kidnapped by these psychos, but I don't understand it, and I never will. Let him sit in the HQ and play politician—I'll find her myself.

And over my dead body will I hand her over to him when I bring her home. She deserves better.

So, I keep pushing, keep searching, with nothing for company but the occasional crackle of the radio hooked to my belt, and the sound of dry pine needles crunching under my boots.

It's about two hours later—and well past sunset, when I'm supposed to report back in—when something oddly shiny reflects back from my headlamp near the base of a tree and catches my eye. I squat down, moving aside pine needles and a stone, to reveal the rest of it. A slim, black pocketknife.

I pick it up and stand, then shove it into my pocket with a sigh. It's the first thing I've found out of the ordinary, sure. But it doesn't lead me any closer to finding Demy, or Nell, or any of the rest of the women I'm sure they're being held with.

I take a step back, rubbing my tired eyes and grumpily wondering if I shouldn't turn in for the night, and start back fresh tomorrow.

Picking up the radio, I press the button to call in. "Hey, Glitch. You still up?"

"You know it. I run on copious amounts of caffeine, electricity, and three-point-five hours of sleep per night."

The man should not be allowed to be that chipper under the kind of stress we are in right now, but that's him. Irrepressible.

"I hear ya. Listen, can you ping my current location?"

"Yes. Your radio is equipped with advanced satellite tracking technology. I can mark the exact location within twenty-five feet."

"Great. Do that for me?"

"Already done. Did you find something of note, or just want to start back there in the morning?"

"Just a lost pocketknife. But it's more than I've found the last few days, so—"

"Every little clue counts. Did you touch it? If it's not contaminated we can have it fingerprinted overnight, see if we come up with any IDs."

Shoot. Why didn't I think of that?

"Uh, yeah I did touch it, but not the blade or the lock. So, you might still get something."

"Excellent. Well, you're all pinged and ready to get back. But maybe carve an X on the tree or something with your *own* knife—twenty-five feet in circumference isn't an insignificant number of trees."

"Will do. Thanks, Glitch."

I definitely needed to head in. My brain was foggy, and I was missing things. I had to be sharp, or I'd miss something important.

My own silver pocketknife—dented and dinged from years of use in the backwoods, much like these—was in my hand and open before I looked up, and when I did, I nearly dropped it.

Holy hell.

Right there, in the trunk of the tree, was a fresh carving, with sap just beginning to ooze out of it.

Lance + Flora.

There was some funky linework around it instead of a heart, but I couldn't get past that name.

Flora, my childhood best friend. My would-be match, whose spirit was broken by the world we live in, and unrelenting old men who didn't care about anything but money.

It wasn't a common name, and there was only one person I'd told that story to, ever.

Demy.

The radio was back in my hand in a flash. "Glitch, I've got something. Send backup, send anybody who's awake and will come. Atlas for sure. I'm close."

Wait. I took a step closer and squinted at the marks around the names. The sap was obscuring it somewhat, but was that an arrow?

"On it, but tell me what you've got so I can prep everyone, and Atlas is right here. I've put you on the intercom so everyone in the control room can hear you."

"I believe Demy left me a message carved into this tree, and it's fresh. Not scabbed over, with just a small amount of sap coming out of the cuts. No crystallization."

"How do you know it's her?" Atlas's tone is all business, but I swear there's a hint of excitement behind the words.

"There's an arrow worked into the carving. And the name . . . it's from a story I told her. My childhood best friend."

"We're coming. Do *not* move from your position without backup, are we clear? There have been no signs of anti-aircraft weaponry in the quadrant you're standing in, which means if you're as close as you think, there may be patrols on foot." Atlas orders, the sounds of him running coming through with the words.

Glitch cuts in—"In case there are patrols nearby, I'm locking your radio onto silent broadcast mode. That means we'll hear everything from your end, but you won't be able to hear us. Help is twenty plus minutes out by ATV, and then by foot when they're close. Stay safe, man. Glitch, out."

The radio leaves eerie silence in its wake, and I check my watch. Half an hour.

A few seconds tick past, and I scan the area, looking for any sign of a patrol. I don't see any, not even deer paths worn into the undergrowth. If they're patrolling on foot, it's either not here or they're extremely careful about not leaving a footpath.

I make a split second decision, carve a heavier arrow on the side of the tree in the direction I'm heading, dim my headlamp, and keep moving.

Demy's close, and backup's on the way. That's good enough for me.

CHAPTER TWENTY-SEVEN

RISK AND REDEMPTION

DEMY

"You stupid, stupid little girl," Lee snarls, slamming me into the wall with his death grip on my arm. "You did that on *purpose.*" His breath is hot and sour in the enclosed space, and I only half catch myself to lessen the impact.

I'm less worried at the moment about adding another bruise to my growing collection than his fury, and the fact that I'm alone.

Why did I drop that knife? I should have known he'd be pissed off.

"I didn't! I tripped. I'm so sorry," I insist, raising my voice in the hope that this hall isn't deserted, and maybe someone will come to redirect his ire.

"Sorry? I'd *just* assured Benji I was out for a post-rotation smoke. And then here you come, stumbling out and making a liar out of me!" He shakes me so hard my teeth knock together.

I stiffen my muscles, trying to lessen the jarring, dizzying impact the best I can without blatantly attacking him back.

Would it matter? He's so angry he might actually kill me this time. My heart is in my throat, and I'm struggling to think of what else to say to back him off. "I'm sorry" doesn't seem to be doing anything.

"I would never, Lee! Please, you have to believe me!"

"Believe you? I should have finished what I started the other day, and rid this world of another nuisance female! Instead, I tried to make nice, and instead of getting laid, I got *screwed!*" A glob of his spit flies off his lip right along with the vitriolic words, and lands on my cheek. But when I reach up to wipe it away, he knocks my hand aside.

I can't help but cry out at the hit, which sends my elbow ricocheting off the rough cement walls.

"Lee, I'm sorry. I'm so sorry!"

"Not yet, but you will be."

His promise sends a cold spiral of dread corkscrewing through my middle, but I don't have time to think, because he's dragging me down the hallway. Instead of going back towards the cells, though, I'm pulled right off the main hallway and into a dimly lit storage closet. There are a few racks on the wall, but my blood runs cold when I see the dirty, stained mattress in the back corner.

No, *no, no, no . . .*

"Lee, please don't do this. I— I—"

He backhands me, right across the cheek. Blood flies across the boxes of supplies, leaving my lip throbbing and my ears ringing from the impact.

I stagger backwards a step, trying my hardest not to look at the door he didn't bother to open. *Clearly* he's not worried about anyone stopping him, but if I can distract him long enough to make a run for it, I can get lost in the tunnels.

I've been running from these abusers for a third of my life; I can hang on a few more days until help comes.

The decision grounds me, sucks away all distractions, like I'm back on the mats, sparring under Peter's tutelage. There's nobody but me, and my attacker. I bounce up on the balls of my feet, staying light and watching for signs he's about to attack again.

"Take off your dress," he orders, pointing to the corner where he wants me to toss it.

"No. I won't." I lift my chin and glare at him. The madder he gets, the better a chance he has of slipping up, making a mistake.

"You will, or I'll tear it off you," he snarls, taking a threatening step towards me.

I take a half-step back, trying not to bump the wall, but angling my back towards the door. A big jug of bright yellow cleaning fluid catches my interest from the corner of my eye, but he sees what I'm trying to do and lunges between me and the open doorway.

Crap.

I dance out of his way, more sluggish than I'd like after having my bell rung by his slap, but still out of reach.

"Fight all you want. I like it when girls are feisty."

"Yeah? Well I like it when jerks like you get what's coming to them." I don't wait for him to respond. I lunge for the wire shelf on the side wall, grabbing the first thing my hand lands on. It's a midsized wet/dry vacuum, with a shiny metal body canister. I grab it by the handle and keep turning, swinging with my whole body.

He lunges forward, but I catch him with the vacuum, right at rib height.

He swears and jumps back, putting himself in the doorway so I can't catch him on the side again. But I brandish my weapon with a fierce scowl.

158

"Let me out of here!"

"Over my dead body, you *bit—*" His words are cut off as a hulking shadow of a man appears in the hall behind him, locking him up in a chokehold.

I blink once, again, and then recognition hits me like an electric train, and a grateful sob tears itself out of my throat.

"Fletcher?" The muscles in his forearms could be etched from marble, they're so sharply defined as he wrestles the still-struggling Lee into the storeroom. He doesn't answer me at first, focused on Lee, who's trying to claw his way free of Fletcher's grip.

One of Lee's hands drops, fumbling with his cloak, and I remember the second, larger knife he's got inside his belt.

"Not today, you prick!" I swing the vacuum again, bashing into Lee's hand with a satisfying *crack* of metal on bone.

The hand falls, limp, as his oxygen finally runs out. Fletcher drags his limp frame to the corner mattress, dropping him unceremoniously and pulling out a zip tie from his own utility belt. He snatches the man's arms behind his back, zip-ties them together, then repeats the motion with his feet. When it's all said and done, he runs one more tie between his feet and hands, pulling it so tight he's going to wake up in a world of hurt.

When he turns to me, it's with equal parts shock and relief on his handsome face. His eyes are warm as he holds up his hands, palms open as if I'm a skittish horse he wants to gentle.

"I'm here, it's going to be okay," he says, but I'm already throwing myself at him, tears threatening as I try not to get crushed under a mountain of emotions as his familiar woodsy, masculine scent envelops me.

"Shhh, we're not out of the woods yet. Help is on the way, though. Let me get you out of here, and then we can bring in the cavalry to get Nell."

That snaps me out of it quickly. "I'm not leaving without her."

"We are *not* leaving her here. But I can't concentrate on finding her if I have to watch both of our backs, please. Let's get out of this hallway—the exterior door is close—and backup will be here in minutes."

I bite my lip, not at all liking the idea of stepping into freedom without Nell, not even for five seconds.

"I promise you, Demy," he says, holding my gaze steady. And I see it there, the fierce determination, the promise.

"Okay. But only *right* outside. I'm not letting you cart me off to safety while she's still in here."

"I wouldn't dream of it." He squeezes me tight to his chest for another second, like he's memorizing me, before making quick work of stripping the weapons off Lee's belt. "What do you want?" He holds up a pistol, a police-style metal baton, and the big black buck knife.

I think for a second, then grab the knife and the pistol. I pull up the dress hem and slide the knife into the thigh pocket of my exercise pants. The gun I keep in my hands, pointed at the floor. He slips the baton through an empty loop in his own belt, and then leads the way to the door.

"Stay right behind me, and if you see anything moving, shoot first. These sickos are *all* guilty."

"Yes they are," I agree, and then we're moving into the dark hallway.

It feels like every hair on my body stands on end as we move as silently as possible towards the bunker door. Any minute, the boogeyman is going to leap out, brain Fletcher, and throw me back into the cell.

Or worse, this will all have been a fever dream, the product of an overactive imagination after getting backhanded.

But we reach the door without incident, and I hold my breath as Fletcher grabs the handle.

"Wait! There was a guard on patrol. Benji," I add, as if that helps him ward the man off somehow. Who knows, I'm clearly delirious from everything that's happened today.

"Chubby guy, medium height, green eyes?"

"I didn't pay attention to his eye color while he was dragging me back into this cesspit, but probably?"

He snorts a laugh at my sarcasm. "I already took care of him. He's sporting a goose egg and a pair of plastic wrist accessories behind a tree about ten yards that way." He points towards the tree bench, and I grin.

"Well let's get the heck out of here," I say.

Fletcher works the door open with an impressive display of muscle—the same door Lee had struggled to open—quickly checking for any sign of a guard before waving me through. When the cool air bathes my face this time, it hits differently. I'm embarrassed at the tears trying to overwhelm me again, yet helpless to stop it.

Freedom. Sweet, blessed freedom.

"Come on, the cavalry should be coming from this direction." He grabs my hand with his left, his own pistol held in the other.

We jog quietly for a few minutes, until we see lights bobbing in the distance. He stops in his tracks and pulls me behind a tree, placing his body in front of mine as he peers around. Instead of stifled, though, I feel *safe*, and to my shame a sob of relief breaks free. I stifle it with my palm, not wanting to alert the Cabal to our hiding place if that's who's coming.

"I have Demy, and we're outside the bunker. I see lights approaching. If they're friendly, flash twice," he says in a low voice, speaking to seemingly no one.

But twenty tense seconds later, the lights all flash twice. He slides his gun back into its holster and scoops me into his arms. And then he's running, straight towards our reinforcements.

CHAPTER TWENTY-EIGHT

REUNION

FLETCHER

I did it. She's safe. Relief, hot and tangible, pulses through my veins as I set her down in the midst of the horde of men who came to back me up. We're still in the trees, so I position her in front of one, and put myself between her and the crowd. She's eyeing them with a mix of wariness and relief. I keep one arm on the rough bark, not touching her but close enough to feel the warmth radiating off her skin. Because she's alive.

She's been through hell and back, but she's alive.

The words are running on repeat like a tattoo inside my skull.

She's alive. She's alive. Alive.

Atlas nearly bowls into me, sprinting to our position behind the tree. He zooms in on Demy, eyes like lasers. I press my free hand to his chest, stopping him from crowding into her space. He ignores it, focused on one thing, and one thing only.

"Where's Nell? Tell me everything you remember about the layout." He's studying her face, every twitch, every hitch of her breath.

"There are a few turns between the exit door and where they're keeping the women. I don't know which cell Nell's in, because she wasn't my roommate. She's still wearing the same clothes, and all of the women are kept on the same aisle. The cell doors . . . they're clear, but it's nighttime so all the lights are dimmed and *will* be for . . . I don't know. A while? I'm not sure if they keep the same schedule inside as the sun does outside."

She presses a shaking hand to her forehead.

"That's good, Demy. That's enough," I soothe, but she shoots me a dagger-like look.

"It's not. I'm coming with you. I promised her I wouldn't leave her behind, and I keep my promises."

"Absolutely not. No." I try not to let my anger get the best of me, but the idea of her walking right back into danger—possibly losing her, now, at the finish line? It's unconscionable to me.

"You don't get to decide that, Fletcher. And as grateful as I am, this is not about you."

"No, it's not. It's about *you*. I love you, and I can't bear to risk your life again, not after I've just snatched you out of the lion's jaws. Please, Demy. Tell us everything. I'll give you my radio so you can give Atlas directions. But *please* don't make me watch you go back through those doors."

Her lower lip trembles, a tortured look on her face as her gaze swivels to Atlas. "I can't leave her, I can't. She's . . ."

Atlas offers a big, meaty paw, palm up. She rests her delicate one in his, slowly meeting his eyes. "If you need to do this, I will have you suited up in body armor in ninety seconds, and we'll roll. But if there's any way you're willing to stay safely outside, I've got a helmet cam, and a radio receiver in my left ear. I will give you the command tablet, where you can watch my helmet feed, and give me directions from right here. And when—*when*—I've got Nell safely in my arms? I'll carry her straight to you, and tell her what you did for her. She won't begrudge you this, Demy. I know my wife. But you've got forty-five seconds to decide, and then we breech with or without you."

The man is cool as a cucumber, as he holds her gaze. It's the confidence of a man who knows he's about to win the gold medal. Take the last shot, and sink it. He was born for this moment. And she sees it, just as much as I do.

"Give me the tablet."

I blow out a relieved breath as Atlas whips a large, crystal-clear tablet in a black tactical case from his backpack and taps twice to show Demy's own face reflected from his helmet cam.

"It's not mirrored, so if I need to go left, say left. If you're unsure, say that too. I've got backup. Now, twenty seconds left before we get into breech formation—tell me every single thing you remember about the cell block, and how many captives are inside.

"I'd guess there are . . . fifty or so women. The cells are pretty simple. There's a door on every single one, with a latch above head height only accessible from the outside. There is a metal gate, which one of the guards has a key to. I don't know if there's another way to open it."

"How did the man you were with get you out?" I ask, hesitant to interrupt.

"I— I don't know. He didn't open it after getting me out of the cell, or lock it back afterward."

"So, it may be open. Thank you, Demy, for everything you've done for my wife. I'll never forget it. You've got a guard of six. If there's any sign of trouble, getting Demy to safety is your number one priority. Do not follow us, under any circumstances." He meets my eyes at that last line, and I nod solemnly.

As much as I've grown to respect Atlas, he doesn't have to worry about me following him in. I meant what I said. I love Demy, and I will move heaven and earth to keep her safe every day for the rest of her life, if she'll let me.

Atlas gives a "circle up and head out" hand signal, and most of the headlamps click into dim mode, then trail after him towards the bunker entrance. Demy's eyes are already fixed on the tablet, but I stay cautious, keeping my position in front of her, and making sure there's no unexpected interference while we're all looking somewhere else. It's not until the last six NAA police officers peel off from the line and form up around the two of us to stand guard during the attack that I breathe a little easier.

Demy and I have got a highly trained human shield wearing full tactical body armor, and the Cabal isn't going to know what hit them when Atlas breeches with his team.

I shift to the side so that I can see the helmet feed right side up, then Demy and I watch in tense silence as the bunker door comes into view.

Atlas's hand moves, and one of the men runs forward, placing small devices on the inset hinges. I brace for a boom, but I hear only a small fizzing sound —no more than cracking open a two-liter bottle of soda, and a thin trail of smoke wafts up from each device. A second motion, and it takes four men to lift the door free from where it's set into the ground.

"Oh my God, this is really happening, isn't it? This isn't a dream?" Demy's voice is lighter than air, but the feeling of her hand on my forearm is solid. I place my own hand over it, giving her a small squeeze now that she's initiated the contact.

"It's real. It's about to all be over." I whisper the reassurance, not wanting to distract Atlas or anyone else by chattering over the operations radio channel.

Atlas is already halfway down the dark staircase to the ground level of the bunker. He clears each room before passing the doorway, and I'm surprised that there are only two guards in one room. They're tased and zip-tied before they know what hit them—probably thanks to the multiple empty beer cans littering the table and the ground around their chairs.

He stops at the corner, risking a quick glance in each direction to ensure the way is clear.

"Any guidance, Demy?" His voice is low, barely audible over the radio.

"I think it's right. Also, Lee told me it's past curfew, so in *theory* anyone who's not on guard should be asleep," she says, then hesitates. "But I don't know if he was telling me the truth."

"Roger that."

He gestures again—something only half caught by his helmet feed, then we see some of the forces branch to clear the left side of the bunker before he starts down the hall to the right.

Every door he passes, if it's open, he clears. If it's shut, he pulls a glob of black, sticky goo and smears it into the crack between the frame and the door. Some sort of sealant? I'll ask him later.

Everything is going seamlessly until he makes it to the next crossroad.

"I'm not sure about this one. I'm so sorry. There's an open gathering area near the cell block, too. Any time we passed their communal space, there were *always* people in it."

He gives his camera a silent thumbs up, then after scanning each side hall, heads straight.

167

The helmet cam starts to pick up noise, which must be why he chose this direction. He skids to a stop, and for the first time, we hear gunfire. Black-cloaked figures rush toward him, flashes from his muzzle lighting the screen and sending it nearly white in the exchange. Dust from chunks blown out of the concrete walls fills the air amid the sounds of grunts and thuds, screams and bellows.

When the cacophony dies and the dust settles, we're looking at an empty gathering area, nothing but men in pools of black fabric draped on the floors. Some are raising their hands overhead in surrender, as Atlas's men circulate and zip-tie them up one by one. In seconds, though, he's back on the move. The camera spins with dizzying speed, and then I see it.

The line of cells, the metal gate locked up tight. But my heart nearly explodes with horror when it focuses on the man standing a few feet behind it, and the diminutive, bruise-covered woman in his arms being used as a human shield.

"Oh, God, Nell!" Demy sobs. "I'm so sorry, Nell, I should be in there! I *should be in there!*" Demy tries to shove past me, but I bracket her in. It kills me to restrain her after all she's been through, but the *last* thing Atlas needs right now is a distraction in the form of a pissed-off and terrified Demy barreling into the mix.

"Shh, Demy. He's going to get her."

"That bastard Manuel has a gun to her cheek! Let me go, let me go!"

"Hush, now." I try to soothe her. "He doesn't need us freaking out in his ear right now. All we can do is wait."

The stark reminder of us being in Atlas's ear makes her fall immediately silent, and whip the tablet back up, even as tears streak down both of her cheeks. Every muscle in my body is tight enough to snap, but I keep it together—I have to.

"You have three minutes to get every single one of your men out of this bunker, or this one gets the top of her pretty blonde head blown off," Manuel says, voice cold as ice and as sharp as a dagger.

"He used to act so kind . . . benevolent, even. I guess when the rubber meets the road, that pretense is long gone," Demy whispers, bitter venom dripping from the quiet words.

I squeeze her arm and watch, unable to look away even as I think I *should turn this tablet off.*

If anything goes wrong, or happens to Nell, Demy will never get those images burned out of her brain.

Please, don't let anything go wrong. I send up a silent prayer, wrapping my arm around Demy's shoulder in a grateful squeeze.

Atlas is silent, and no hand gestures show on the camera, even though I hear the thud of boots forming up on either side of him.

"I mean it! Every last man *out*, or she gets it."

Another long, silent pause from Atlas, and the man raises his voice. "Now! Or you can kiss your wife goodbye."

"Nell-Bell? I'm not going to let anything happen to you," Atlas murmurs, the words only for her.

Nell sobs but keeps her eyes locked on Atlas. Demy's tears are silent streams on her own cheeks as she rides through this with her friend. But Nell's got this look in her eyes . . . terror, yes, but *trust.* Everything inside me feels like it's cracking in half, for both women. For everything about this sick situation.

She can't get hurt. She just can't, not this close. None of us would survive it.

"Get out!" The man's voice cracks with hysteria on the end of the word, hand shaking on the gun that's digging painfully into Nell's cheek. His finger's on the trigger, and I feel like I might vomit. The deranged idiot could shoot her on *accident*.

"Bathtub!" Atlas barks the word, and everything seems to happen at once. Nell goes limp in the man's arms, there's the crack of a gun firing, and Demy screams, the sound ear piercing as I sway on my feet.

CHAPTER TWENTY-NINE

RICOCHET

DEMY

No. Someone's screaming. Is it me? I don't know, and I don't care. Nell just fell, limp as a rag doll. But when I open my eyes, through the blur of tears I see that Manuel fell, too. There's some sort of struggle happening, but everything starts shaking violently on the camera, and it's hard to tell what's going on.

"Is she dead? Just tell me if she's dead, Fletcher, I can't look." The words are acid on my tongue. I left her. It's my fault. Nausea swamps me. I shouldn't have agreed to leave her. Maybe I'd have been the one behind that gun, and Atlas would have been able to think clearly.

Not poor Nell.

It's my worst nightmare, come to life. Not only did I get captured by the Cabal, but they swept up my dearest friend right along with me. And now she's paid the ultimate price for my strangeness. My *wrongness*.

God, it should have been me.

He gently pries the tablet from my stone fingertips, and the silence is deafening.

"Look, Demy. Just look," he urges, holding it in front of my face. So, I do, bracing myself for the worst.

But it's not. Oh, thank every god who'll listen, *it's not*. Nell's up and running to Atlas. They crash together, the jolt to his helmet cam making me a little motion sick, but I don't care. I'm so relieved, it's a physical *squeeze* inside my chest.

"She's alive. Oh, she's okay. Nell!" I burst into tears, burying my face into Fletcher's chest. Relief mixing with the adrenaline pounding through my veins. I clutch onto him like a spider monkey, but he clutches me right back, passing the tablet off to one of our guards, and then he's holding me, safe and close.

When the tears slow, I look up at his face, so handsome in the moonlight.

"Thank you, Fletcher. For every single thing. You—" I clear my throat, thick with tears. "You didn't give up on me. You could have. I wouldn't have blamed you—"

He shakes his head. "I couldn't give up on the woman I love any more than I could my next breath. I missed you, Demy. Even if you're not ready, or don't feel the same way—I love you, and I'm going to tell you as many times as you need to hear it. "

His words settle in like feathers, floating down to coat every surface of my brain.

He loves me. He *came for me*. He risked his own life to pull me out of that cesspit. I just hug him again, lost for words. I'll need to find some, eventually, but not right now. With his arms around me, everything inside settles, falling into place. Even without the words, *he knows*.

"Demy?" The voice is thin, but excited. I rip myself out of Fletcher's arms, and he lets me go. Our guards part, and there she is.

"Nell, oh, I'm so sorry! I shouldn't have let them drag me out here without you. I was so scared." I'm crying again, my tears leaking like a faucet as I run to her, and she meets me halfway.

We crash together, bones creaking. It's no gentle meeting of friends, it's a physical car crash, but I love every second. I squish her to me like she's going to vanish, and she squishes me right back.

"You're going to have to tell me everything. I hear you've been through a lot tonight?" She pulls back, that motherly concern on her face making me laugh.

"I'll tell you, but not right now. Right now I want to get out of these woods, out of these *clothes*—heck. Can you guys take us out of the tri-state? Somewhere far, *far* from these sickos," I beg.

"She's got a point." Nell loosens her grip to turn and smile up at Atlas. "Let's get everybody else out of there, and go home."

Chapter Thirty

AFTERSHOCKS

Demy

The reality of getting the rest of the women out of the bunker and dealing with all of the men from the Cabal who need to be questioned, processed, and detained isn't so simple, and they can't ferry us out of the tri-state immediately. But Nell and I are escorted by Fletcher and our six-person guard to the HQ, a large warehouse a few miles away where our rescuers made a temporary base. Meanwhile, Atlas and a specially-trained team of female NAA police officers start freeing the rest of the women, explaining the situation, and prepping them to come to the HQ as well.

There are showers, beds, and a cook who has hot, fresh Belgian waffles and bacon waiting for us as soon as we're clean and changed into spare black fatigues.

There's a strange similarity to the bunker, which makes me shiver, but the company is infinitely better. Within the hour, I've got a full belly, clean hair, and am safely tucked away in a private sitting room. There are couches and throw pillows, a coffee table, and a still in-date stack of glossy magazines off to the side. It's oddly . . . *normal.*

Fletcher, Nell, Atlas, Glitch, and, to my surprise, King Patrick, are all sitting with me.

It's still weird that Nell just . . . knows him. They're old friends, cracking jokes as she's curled in Atlas's lap.

I look around the room, and a realization hits me. "Where's Beckett? Did he make it out okay? They said he'd been ransomed, but . . ." Dread nearly chokes me all over again.

"He's fine," the king says in a wary tone, before flicking a questioning glance at Fletcher.

"We thought you might like a day before talking to anyone else," Fletcher finishes the hanging sentence, giving my hand a squeeze in the process.

"He's here, too?"

"He is," Fletcher says, as if the words are dog crap on his tongue. I can tell he doesn't want to say it, and I'm confused. They didn't get along per se, but there wasn't outright animosity between them before I was taken.

Something happened there, and I'll have to ask them eventually.

"We're not going to be talking to *anyone* else until you've been checked out by the doctor. I've called Courso in from Wrightsville. He's the royal family's physician these days . . . and he's used to getting our calls at odd hours. He should be here in the next ninety minutes, give or take."

It's probably wise to get checked out. I ache all over, and Nell looks like she survived a *literal* car crash.

"The other women—are they all here now?"

King Patrick nods. "They're all getting showered and choosing clothes, and we're providing them places to sleep and phones to contact their next of kin." He nods to Glitch. "Glitch has a program running to help find their legal identities, and the most up-to-date information on their relatives. Some of the women have been missing for a very, very long time."

I close my eyes, not surprised but still saddened by the news.

"The doctor should probably check them out, first," Nell says. "One or more of them are recently post-op."

"What kind of operation?" Glitch asks, looking confused. "I found medical records matching each woman's physical description, but nothing that mentioned an operation." He rapidly swipes at his ever-present tablet, brows furrowed into deep lines.

"We don't know. The running speculation was sterilization, but all we know for certain was that it was laparoscopic."

"I— Hmm. Okay, well, I'll keep digging, and we'll let the doctor know."

"You're still getting checked out *first*," Atlas demands, clutching Nell a little tighter against his chest.

"Okay, okay—I'll be a good patient so long as you promise they all get checked by Dr. Courso tonight, too."

"Anyone who will consent to an exam is welcome to it, now or later, free of charge. Their follow-up medical and mental health care will be completely covered, as well," the King assures her. "But we can't force an exam on traumatized women who don't want one. That makes us no better than the Cabal."

"You might have better luck if this doctor has some female staff," I offer. "Speaking of, did you find a woman in any of the other rooms who wasn't a prisoner? They had a nurse—Annie."

"We found one woman who hasn't spoken to us, or interacted with any of the other women since we pulled her from her room, so it's possible she was the nurse. At the compound, she was sequestered apart from the others in a private cell, and she had a three-year-old daughter with her."

All the blood drains from my face.

"That's awful. Is the little girl okay?" Nell asks, abruptly getting to her feet against Atlas's protests.

She had a daughter in there. I feel nauseated, and simultaneously like the room just turned on its side with all of us in it. So many of the small things about her click into place, suddenly making more sense.

"She appears fine, though very confused about who all of us are and why we're above ground. Based on *her* records . . . she was born in one of their bunkers." His voice is low with the gravity of that statement.

This poor child has lived her entire life a captive in a cell, under-ground. Never feeling the sun on her face, or the wind in her hair. Suddenly I have to say something, even if it makes everyone in the room mad at me.

"She should get an exception. The little girl." I stumble over the words, but make myself look King Patrick in the eye, nonetheless. I learned the hard way that men won't take you seriously if you don't. "She was born into slavery, she shouldn't *ever* have her choices taken away from her again, and that includes the New Lives Program."

You could hear a pin drop in the room, and for a long moment it seems like nobody breathes. Nell watches the interaction with wide eyes, but even she doesn't say a word.

"I agree. We've been working to slowly dismantle the program, working within the bounds of standard government process. But many in Parliament like the program, which has made it a slog to get the mandates fully removed. After this, though . . . it's time to stop playing footsie." He holds my gaze and nods, leaning back in his chair.

"Nobody blames you for this, Patrick," Glitch says, casting a quick glance at me after the fact. "Evil men will always exist. All we can do is keep stomping them out and doing our dead-level best to take away their power to hurt others."

The King nods, but his knuckles are white on the arms of the chair. "I have a responsibility to do more than that, though. I'm responsible for every single citizen on this *continent*. But there's no manual for situations like these." He runs a hand through his thick, black hair, before letting it drop back onto the arm of the chair.

"We're with you, you know that," Nell says, patting him lightly on the shoulder before settling back onto Atlas's lap like a bird in a nest. I swallow down an uncharacteristic pang of jealousy when his arms go around her so easily, so *surely*. They fit together like puzzle pieces, made to be, and cut from the same cloth, despite their differences.

My situation still feels complex, unsettled. And after what I've been through . . . I sneak a glance at Fletcher from the corner of my eye, but he catches me. A soft smile curls the corner of his lips, and he doesn't move, save to curl his fingers around mine in a comforting squeeze that sends tingles through every part of me.

But in the back of my mind, I can't let go of the thought that Beckett is somewhere in this building, also recovering from his own kidnapping, and that it's wrong to be this cozy with Fletcher while he's still in limbo.

While all *three* of us are.

And then a question plays through my head, that I know I'm not going to be able to let go of any time soon.

Why did you fight for the little girl's choices, and not your own?

CHAPTER THIRTY-ONE

COURSO AND . . .

DEMY

"**I**'m sorry, I'm going to need you to repeat that, doc."

Doctor Courso doesn't laugh, despite Nell's gobsmacked expression, or irreverent response. "Of course. I said, you have an abnormally high number of ovarian follicles, as if you underwent a round of stimulating drugs."

Nell's typical brash tone turns into a semi-hysterical laugh as she clutches Atlas's hand. "Are you telling me that the whole time I thought those psychopaths were preparing to spay me like a stray dog, they were in fact pumping me full of super-baby juice to *harvest my eggs*?"

Though his eyebrows shoot up at the question, after a moment to think it over, he nods. "It appears so. The laparoscopic surgery is a bit of a head scratcher, because typically retrieval is all done transvaginally, but it's possible they didn't have the proper surgical equipment to achieve that. I really can't say unless we have more information, or surgical records. But to answer your initial question, not only are you still fertile, you'll need to be careful this cycle unless you want an *extremely* high chance of multiple pregnancy."

"Multiples as in . . . ?" a very pale Atlas asks.

"Naturally, twins or, rarely, triplets are possible. With this many follicles, octuplets aren't unheard of from historical studies, though I can't advise that you try for that. That many at once results in substantially more risk, highly complicated pregnancies."

"Holy sh—"

I grab Nell's hand, stopping her mid-swear. "No babies this month, Nell. You need time to recover, okay? Promise me."

She nods, wide-eyed as the doctor turns to me. "Would you like an exam? I can do a basic physical if you're not imminently concerned about your fertility status. And I can also refer you to several great gynecologists who'd be happy to handle your follow-up care, if you'd be more comfortable with that."

"I really think I'm all right," I mutter, blushing because I'm a little wigged by a complete stranger—even a doctor—asking about my baby box in front of Atlas. At least at the NLC, you knew they were basically a baby assembly line, and used to the topic. This guy? I don't know him from Adam.

"So, you're declining to consent to an exam?" he asks gently, not pressuring me either way. He's not the creepy Cabal doctor, and I know that. Every second of this experience screams *consent*, and I appreciate it, I do. *It's just so fresh.*

"Demy . . ." Nell's voice is all motherly censure. She's really going to rock as a mom one of these days.

"No, it's fine. You can check me out. But I'm good on the, uh, gyno part. Thanks."

He nods and pulls on a fresh pair of gloves. "Let me clean the exam table and then you can hop up."

I nod, holding Nell's hand a little too tightly while I wait my turn to be poked and prodded. Anxiety is ripping through my system, the bad memories of underground med facilities far too fresh for this. Nell reminded me about not only tonight's abuse, but also of getting choked nearly to death just a few days ago, and I know I should let him check me.

Thankfully, I have a friend who's willing to stay with me, even though I'm sure she's just as bogged down by the memories as I am.

It was only a few weeks, our time inside, and yet somehow it feels like the Cabal grabbed hold of the river that was my life and bent it, sending me along a path I was never meant to be on.

Though maybe they did that when I was a child, and I'm only just realizing the true effects of that. The thought makes me sad as I climb onto the exam table and close my eyes.

"Okay, Demy, let's look at these bruises and see if there's anything I can do for you." Doctor Courso's voice is gentle, but I still jump when his gloved hand gently touches the ugly bruises on my neck.

Fletcher is waiting outside the makeshift exam room, which isn't really surprising. But so is Beckett, and that fact sends me into an immediate spiral. Another person whose life I completely derailed, immediately on the back of the stressful medical exam—I've got a suspected cracked rib, and two likely broken bones in my left hand, where it hit the concrete wall earlier—and I'm done. Just *done* with everything.

"I— I can't do this right now. I'm so sorry." My voice cracks on the sorry, and Nell is at my side, glowering at the two men before us in an instant.

"Did you two *really* think now was the time for this? Atlas, get rid of them." Nell doesn't wait for a response, simply loops her arm through mine, and pulls me away from the men.

"Demy, wait!" Fletcher calls past Atlas's imposing bulk, and Nell pauses, looking over at me to see what I want to do. I just close my eyes against the very unwelcome tears I can feel building behind my eyelids. A near-imperceptible shake of my head, and she leads me away towards my temporary sleeping quarters, letting the hurt feelings and unpleasant decisions wait for another day.

CHAPTER THIRTY-TWO

. . . CONSEQUENCES

FLETCHER

"You could've done the honorable thing and let me have a moment alone to speak with her, you know," Beckett has the *nerve* to gripe once Nell has whisked Demy fully out of earshot. "She wouldn't have minded if there was only one of us here, and you've already had significantly more time with her since she was rescued."

"Are you *serious* right now? I'm here because you're a narcissistic jerk who couldn't wait until tomorrow to ambush her, and I didn't want her to have to deal with you alone, right after the doctor, which probably *upset her*."

Beckett turns angrily in my direction, fists clenched at his side like he wants to throw a punch.

Bring it, Beckett. I didn't get to punch nearly enough people tonight. Atlas agrees with me, but the NAA police took over almost as soon as he extracted Nell, and they insisted on *proper booking procedures.*

Basically, a BS reason not to punch a lot of very deserving faces in, if you ask me. But every single man was being processed into a temporary holding facility less than a mile down the road, while they were questioned and readied to transport to a real penitentiary. It itched to have them all so close to Demy, but the place was being run tighter than a submarine, and crawling with NAA police.

"Cool it, both of you. It's been a very long night for all of us, and both of you are stupider than you look if you think this is the way to win her over," Atlas says with an exasperated roll of his shoulders. "I plan on spending the rest of the night with my wife—and if you two do *anything* to bother that girl tonight and mess that up for me, I will bash your skulls together, and I won't even feel sorry about it. Clear?"

"Crystal," I say, trying to keep the sour note out of my voice. I want nothing more than to spend the night holding Demy, but I won't push if she's not ready.

But I'm also not going to let her choose freaking *Beckett* who cares more about his image than he does her.

No way.

She doesn't have to choose me; but she sure as hell can't choose the political virtuoso who's turning their kidnapping into a publicity stunt. If I see him shake one more person's hand, I'm going to break it off.

Okay, I'm going to be *tempted* to break it off, but restrain myself because Demy wouldn't want that.

With a frustrated sigh, I head the opposite direction down the hall, back to the control room, to talk to Glitch and see how the other women are doing, and if he needs any help with anything. Anything to keep my mind off of where I want to be—with Demy.

The next morning I'm grumpy, tired, and to top it off, I smell. They asked all of the men to avoid the shower area last night so the women could be more comfortable, which we were all happy to do. But I admit the full day of grime is sitting badly this morning and adding to my sour mood.

Which is *nothing* compared to what those poor women have endured, so I'm keeping my mouth shut, and heading for caffeination at double speed.

Nearly half of the women have already been removed from HQ, some to the nearest hospital after their exams with Dr. Courso, and a few even to family who were easy to locate and thrilled to get news of their missing family members.

There are at least fifteen left, though, and my wrist comm dings with a reminder of which areas to avoid unless you're female personnel with clearance. Thankfully, the coffee pot is full, and not on the list. I've just poured myself a cup in the little out-of-the-way room when a door across the hall slams open.

Beckett storms out, a stern-faced Patrick sitting at a table inside the room. I hide a smirk behind my coffee cup, and step into the hallway.

"Everything okay out here? You seem awfully hot and bothered for the early hour." I meet Beckett's gaze and then Patrick's, letting my facial expression do most of the talking.

"You know full well it's *not*, you bastard. Well, you win. Good luck with your new wife."

That catches me off guard. "I— What, now?" I ask, genuinely confused.

He closes the distance between us in a nanosecond, grabbing the front of my shirt before thinking better of it and letting go. He swipes his palm over his pristine, pressed pant leg before sneering. "You two deserve each other. Frankly, I can't believe I didn't see it."

"See what?" I genuinely have no idea what could have changed overnight to change his intentions of pursuing Demy—not that I'm mad to have him out of the way.

Patrick looms in the doorway. "Keep your voice down, and if you can't be civil, get out. Your assistance hasn't been needed for more than a week, and if you're officially withdrawing your suit of Demy, you're no longer authorized to be part of these rescue proceedings."

Atlas ambles around the corner, a pissed-off expression on his face.

"My father is going to hear about this. You should have notified me *immediately*, given the reputational risk not only to me, but to our family enterprise. Expect a call from our legal team first thing Monday."

Patrick snorts, the bored noise oddly incongruous with his regal bearing. "Good luck with that."

"Okay, is anybody going to actually fill me in? Not that I'm upset for less competition, here—"

"Competition?" Beckett throws up his hand and scoffs. "As if *anybody* in their right mind wants a genetically modified *experiment* for a wife."

I don't think, I just lunge. My coffee is gone, the paper cup rolling down the hallway on its side forgotten as I swing straight at his smug, demeaning expression. My fist meets his jaw with a satisfying *crack*, but somebody grabs me from behind and hauls me off him before I can get in a second swing.

"You're a coward, Beckett. Go back to Daddy and hide behind his skirts. *You don't deserve her.*"

"That's just *rich*, coming from the man who's shirked all his obligations for years." Beckett holds up a warning finger as he spits a bloody glob of saliva right on the polished white floors. "You can expect a call from my legal team regarding this *assault* come Monday, as well. And in front of an NAA police officer, to boot. Good luck wiggling out of this one." He smiles then, enjoying the idea of causing me trouble as I look over my shoulder to see it's not Atlas who's grabbed me, but Peter. Apparently he was called as part of the escort to see Beckett on his way.

I swallow a groan at the complication his office adds to the whole mess, but I don't regret it. I've got my own legal team, and if he wants to swing his daddy's money around like a club, I can do the same.

"You keep Demy's name out of your mouth, and we won't have any more problems," I say.

"Happily."

"Let's go. You heard the King," Atlas orders, and Beckett turns on his heel and follows him. I don't breathe a normal breath until he's out of sight and Peter lets me go.

"Sorry. I probably shouldn't have done that," I murmur, looking a bit sheepishly at both Peter and Patrick.

Peter snorts. "If you hadn't, I would have. And I don't have a billionaire dad to call up. Just a brother-in-law." He shoots a wink at Patrick, who grunts a non-response. "That guy can kick rocks, and I don't blame you for standing up for your lady." To my surprise, he slaps me supportively on the back. "Demy's a good girl, and she deserves much better than that tool."

"Agreed," Patrick says drily. "And I think it goes without saying that we're not going to add this unpleasant skirmish to her already profound stress right now. One of us can tell her that Beckett has decided to withdraw his suit . . . but she doesn't need to know the ugly things that flew out of his mouth."

"Yes, your highness." Peter's got a grin a mile wide as he takes an obnoxiously flamboyant bow, complete with hand waving.

Patrick groans, and steps back into the small conference room without acknowledging his brother-in-law's antics.

Peter chuckles as he meanders off down the hall. "Don't forget to mop up, lover boy!" He throws the jab over his shoulder then pauses. "Next time you see Demy, can you tell her to swing by? I've got something she'll want back."

I nod, curious but still too furious with Beckett to ask.

He gives me a chipper thumbs up before disappearing around the corner.

With a sigh, I look down and realize he's right. The lid popped off my cup on impact, and then it rolled several feet down the hall, trailing coffee helter-skelter across the tiles.

I turn in the opposite direction towards the nearest broom closet, but when I round the corner, I freeze in my tracks.

Because right there in the hallway is Demy, butt planted on the ground with tears tracking down her beautiful, devastated face.

Chapter Thirty-Three

WRECKED

Demy

I wasn't ready to face the remaining women—one of whom is Erin, the one who attacked me—in the man-free dining area the all-female police squad set up. Apparently, they've rescued enough female captives in the last five years due to corruption inside the NLC that there is a full protocol in place for helping the survivors immediately post-trauma.

Clear the area of men, no mandatory doctor exams, free choice of foods, clothing, sleeping arrangements, and showers. It's a great setup . . . if it weren't for my mixed feelings about the women.

So, I'm here, skulking down a hallway I'm not *technically* supposed to be in, in search of caffeine. Nell told me there was coffee over here. Besides, the men who pulled us out of the bunker don't scare me. I know they're good guys, and I'd rather go back to hanging with them, to get a small slice of normalcy back.

Baby steps.

But before I make it to the corner, I hear angry, raised voices. *Familiar ones.*

"As if anybody in their right mind wants a genetically modified experiment for a wife."

Horror fills me, hot and bone deep. Shame comes quickly on its heels, freezing me in my tracks, blotting out the sounds of the scuffle and more shouting.

Genetically modified experiment for a wife.

Beckett. Someone's told him, maybe Fletcher too. I should have, before any of this mess happened. But . . . the words just keep playing in slow-motion in my head. I let my shoulders connect with the wall, needing something solid to ground me. It's not enough, so I slowly sink down, down the wall until I'm seated, and drop my head into my hands.

The last time I saw him before our kidnapping, he was kissing me like it was more important than his next breath. Telling me I knew which decision was right. *Him.* And now—

Breathe in, breathe out.

He—no, *they*—they may not want me anymore. That's just the truth. I can live with that, I suppose. The gaping hole in my chest says otherwise, but I've quite literally just come through hell and back; this won't break me, not after that.

Except . . . It's more like *on top of that.* I'm not over being kidnapped. I'm not *over* the pain and abuse and fear. It's still a living, breathing thing sharing my body with me. It feels like a scab's been ripped off, leaving an oozing wound on my heart which was already shredded.

So, this? Yeah, it could be the straw that breaks my back. Except I don't feel as sturdy as a camel; more like a fragile baby bird who just fell out of the nest on the top limb, and got the stuffing knocked out of her by every single branch on the way down.

When my pounding heart has slowed a fraction, I realize things have gone quieter, the conversation moved a few steps further down. Or have they all left? Is my path clear to the coffee?

I should probably take a few minutes, go clean up and then try this again, with Nell at my side for emotional support. Running into either man right now . . . I'm not up for it. I can't bear to know.

I've already heard how Beckett feels; but to see the disappointment in Fletcher's eyes, after he swooped in and saved me?

That would break me, in a way that I couldn't come back from. Beckett is a flesh wound. Somewhere deep down, I knew he wasn't ever going to truly be happy with *me*. Love me for who I already am, not who he could mold me into.

Fletcher would gut me.

The sound of footsteps makes me jerk my head up. As if I summoned him, there he is. Handsome, even rumpled from sleep.

Please, no. Not right now. Just not right now.

"Demy?" An anguished look paints Fletcher's handsome face as he takes in the tear tracks on my cheeks, which I'm sure are puffy and blotchy. "You shouldn't have had to hear that. I'm so sorry."

He sinks to the floor in front of me, not touching, but close enough for me to get a whiff of his . . . aroma, and I fight to not wrinkle my nose in response. Even though he's less than perfectly fresh, his familiar presence is still comforting.

Fletcher reaches out a hand and then hesitates, the motion leaving a fissure in my heart. This is it. Where he tells me that he likes me as a person, but he can't risk having a modified wife, or modified babies. I squeeze my eyes shut tight, as if that'll make it go away. Make *him* go away.

"Can I hold your hand?" He asks the question softly, not pushing me.

"I doubt you want to, Fletcher. It's okay. I heard . . . enough. You don't have to pretend—" My voice cracks, so I stop trying. I don't have it in me to give him more permission than that, anyways. Not if I'm going to keep what little shreds remain of my dignity.

He reaches forward, tentatively tugging my hand out of the tangle of my limbs I've used to cocoon myself. To my surprise, he twines our fingers together.

"Hey," he whispers. "Look at me. Please?" He runs his warm, calloused thumb over the back of my hand. It's almost teasing. Pulling me out of hiding.

I risk opening my eyes a sliver, looking up at him under my clumpy, wet lashes. He's smiling when he uses his free hand to capture a tear.

"I hope none of these are on my account. Because I'm not going anywhere unless *you* tell me to."

My mouth pops open. I thought that was a thing that only happened in movies, but no. It's true.

"Why would you stay? You could have anyone. You've already been matched multiple times. And I'm . . . damaged goods. Modified. And I wasn't even brave enough to tell you when I found out." That last confession feels somehow the worst of my many, many sins.

Fletcher shakes his head with an exasperated huff. "Being in a relationship doesn't mean you aren't entitled to privacy, or time to process. Was I surprised? Sure. But I imagine you were even more shaken by the news about yourself, and I'm not angry with you for needing to hold that close to the vest for a while. How could I be?" He adjusts his grip on my hand, just enough so that he can slide into place next to me with his back against the wall.

Like he intends to stay. Not leaving, not running, not disgusted, or disappointed.

A candle-flame sized flicker of hope lights inside me. And then I remember, and the flicker goes out.

"You heard Beckett. I don't expect you to stay and give up your future because of me. This is an arranged marriage. I get that. Okay?" I pull my fingers from his, cupping my face in my palms to block him out again. The sadness is too much. Just too much.

"You are just determined not to hear me. So, I will say it as many times as necessary. I am not leaving. I am not *interested* in leaving. Having you taken from me was one of the two worst things that has *ever* happened in my life—and you already know what the other one was. By some profound luck, I got you back. And you must think I'm crazy if I'd just let you go again because of something that happened to you before you were born."

I blink slowly, chancing a glance up at him. Looking for any signs of a *gotcha, I'm out of here!*

But he's serious. Earnest.

"I don't know what to say. They don't know a hundred percent what the modifications will do."

He shrugs. "I guess we'll find out together."

"You can't be so blasé about this! You're in this program to have children, start a family!"

"You want to know a secret?" He grins, the irreverent expression I usually find charming is right this instant making me want to smack him on the arm. "Getting married *is* starting a family. Of two."

"Fletcher, you know what I mean. Kids. Babies. Tiny man-bun boys to climb trees with. You want that."

"I don't actually care if we have boys or girls. I mean, either way we can take them hiking, right?"

I'm not sure whether I'm a foot deeper in love at his genuine openness, or ready to strangle the man for being intentionally obtuse. He will not be deterred or see reason. See how *wrong* I could be for him.

"I'm not normal, Fletcher. Pretending it's not true will only lead to heartache later on down the road."

"Okay, fine. If you insist, we can say that something bad might happen later on. But why would we throw away something great *right now* because of a *maybe* later? And, news flash, Demy, nobody is normal anymore, or we wouldn't need these programs. Basically, everyone's been modified, it's only a matter of how long ago, and how severely we were impacted. I could be the one that prevents us from conceiving; you ever thought about that?"

No. But I'm not going to admit that.

He ducks his head down to my height, forcing me to lock eyes with him. "Would you love me any less if I couldn't give you a baby that was biologically mine?"

"I, well . . . no."

"So why is it so hard for you to accept that I feel the same exact way about you? I choose not to focus on the negative. I choose to hope. And what I hope for . . . is you."

Chapter Thirty-Four

SOMETHING'S MISSING

Demy

Tears clog my throat as I look deep into his brown eyes, practically drowning in the warmth and acceptance I see there. There's nothing but sincerity, and hope, and, yes, love. Even now that the danger has passed, he's still here.

I don't want to push him away anymore. I want to let him in, accept the comfort, the love he's offering. But how can I, on the heels of Beckett taking back every sweet word *he* said, then throwing me out like so much trash?

I have to guard my heart. I squeeze Fletcher's hands in mine, begging him to see in my eyes what I just can't say.

The sad, slow smile on his lips tells me he does, and I have to hope that for now, it's enough.

Fletcher's wrist comm buzzes. "Shoot. Emergency debriefing. You feeling up to it? If not, I can take you to your room first." He looks up, studying me intently.

Why does it always feel like he sees straight down to my soul, past all the layers of defenses I so desperately want to keep up?

"I actually was heading this way for coffee, before . . ."

He sighs. "Yeah, me too. I dropped mine when I punched Beckett in the face. It was worth it, but I need a jolt too. How about we both grab some, then head to the debriefing?" He hops to his feet in a single, smooth motion, extending a hand down to lift me up.

"Deal. Do I look terrible?" I wave towards my cheeks when I'm steady on my feet.

He grins, leaning into my personal space in a way that sends a delicious shiver across my belly. "You couldn't look terrible if you *tried*." He drops a chaste kiss on my cheek but lingers . . . silently asking permission. Permission for *more*, which surprises me.

Am I ready for that?

After everything with Lee . . . But no. I shove that awful man out of my head, slamming the door shut behind him. Fletcher is *nothing* like Lee. And I don't want to let what happened to me pollute the rest of my life. The Cabal has taken enough from me. I'm not going to give them *this*, too.

I reach up, twining my fingers into his messy bun, and pull his lips to mine. I can feel a brief smile against my lips before he gets serious, tugging my hips closer to his. Every little touch sends a million sparks flying through my veins, and by the time he pulls away, I sway after him. We're two magnets, just waiting to slam together for good.

"I could stay here with you all day," he murmurs, panting, and pulls back from me the tiniest fraction, tucking a strand of loose hair behind my ear. "Besides, I promised you coffee, which I must deliver. And *apparently* Peter has something for you, too. I was given strict instructions not to forget."

"Probably best not to tick off the weapons instructor, huh?" I tease.

"Yeah, I'd like to keep all my limbs attached," Fletcher agrees.

I feel lighter as he tucks my hand into the crook of his arm and leads me around the corner.

Five minutes later, we've both got a steaming cup in hand, and I'm somehow lighter as he guides me into the debriefing room. We're the last two, and we squeeze into the last empty seats at the round table. Nell gives me a finger-wave, looking her usual chipper self, aside from the lingering bruises. She's bouncing in the seat between Atlas and Glitch.

Patrick has a grave look on his face as he makes eye contact with each of us individually. "Thank you all for coming so quickly. After today's meeting, I'll be flying back to Georada with Mav. Sadie's due any day now, and I need to be with her from here on out. But first, we have some updates, and some decisions to make. Since you've all been intimately involved in what's happened here, we value your input and any insights you may have. Atlas, can you start us off with an update on the captive women, and then, Peter, any findings from the bunker."

Atlas nods, looking around the room with less gravity than Patrick. "We're moving along well. There are less than ten women left who haven't gone on to their families, their personal homes, or hospital care for the two who needed it."

Am I one of those ten? I don't have a home to go back to, except the NLC . . . The thought of going back to the site of my kidnapping sours my stomach. I take a deep breath and push it aside, making a mental note to talk to Nell about where we're going from here. Atlas is still talking, so I try to pay attention.

"Our recovery teams know their stuff; we haven't had any major issues. There was an altercation yesterday, but it was handled swiftly, and they were separated. We expect by tomorrow evening, everyone will be moving on, and we can dissolve the temporary HQ."

Altercation is a polite way to put it. *Three guesses who that was.* I shudder, subtly rubbing my arms at the memory of the throbbing scratches Erin left etched into my flesh.

"Thank you, Atlas," Patrick says. "That's excellent news. Peter?"

"The bunker is clear of all unfriendlies, and they've been detained. A few had the Maiden's Blush neurotoxin capsules, but raiding during the night cycle on their home turf was a boon because at least eighty percent of their personnel were recovered. It's the largest number of Cabal members we've ever taken for questioning, given their propensity for poisoning themselves."

"Any revelations from the first round of interrogation?"

"Nothing major. Most everyone is still tight-lipped, but that's to be expected in organized crime. The longer they've been separated, the more we'll get. Within the next few days, they're going to be transported to Wrightsville Penitentiary for holding and continued questioning until court. There's enough evidence based on the women alone to put every single man inside away for the rest of their lives."

There's a beat of quiet, the import of those words sinking into our collective conscience. All of those men. My abductors, jailers, attackers . . . all behind bars. For life.

A small, primal part of me wishes they were all dead and six feet under. Dead men can't get free or keep trying to pull strings from jail. But locking them up also seems fitting, given what they did to me. To *us*.

I lock eyes with Nell. Her face is deadly calm, but I can see the vindication in her eyes. It's the *least* of what they deserve. The very, very least.

"Thank you, Peter. Please keep us updated as new intelligence comes to light," Patrick says with a nod. "Glitch, I believe you had the segment which needed the most discussion. Ready to catch us up?"

"Rick-raff, the news isn't good."

A leaden pit forms in my stomach. Glitch is perpetually upbeat—almost inhumanly so—but today he looks frustrated and defeated. He's not even tapping his tablet or rambling.

"That's okay. We're all here to support each other as we untangle this mess. Just because this is a big breakthrough doesn't mean it's an *easy* breakthrough." Patrick squeezes his shoulder in a show of brotherly support.

"Okay. Well . . . you all know there were no surgical records. No records of fertility treatments, despite, uh"—he flips an apologetic look at Nell and seems to change tack mid-sentence—"multiple women who consented to examinations with Doctor Courso were found to have excessively high levels of follicle stimulating hormones in their system. His professional opinion is that the Cabal was for some reason harvesting eggs. But we didn't find anything inside the bunker to support that assumption, aside from the women themselves. I've dug, and I've hacked, and I've got programs running around the clock, but everything I'm throwing at their data is coming up disappointingly empty. There is more to the story here, and either they've buried it extremely well, or we're staring at something big, and missing it."

He taps the table in agitation, a rapid staccato beat, before stopping himself and dropping his hand back into his lap.

A thought occurs to me. "Did you ever find out why they were tracking me? I wasn't given any injections, but they did do a couple of blood tests."

"Nothing new, and nothing conclusive on that front, either," Glitch says, raking a hand through his wild hair. "The best I can say is that every single woman who was missing over four months had laparoscopic surgery in that time, and our first patient workup—shared with permission, of course—shows that the woman was not medically sterilized."

You could hear a penny drop on carpet, it's so quiet.

"Was there physical infrastructure for the storage of genetic material? Coolers, freezers, liquid nitrogen . . . ?" Nell asks, a crinkle between her eyebrows.

"Nothing like that, and we've confirmed every single room has been opened and searched," Peter answers.

"So, let's just go on the assumption for a minute that they were doing these surgeries. What did they do with all the eggs? And is that why they've been keeping the women? I did find medical records of *many* other women who were no longer inside this particular bunker, and each one has been cross-checked against a missing person's list. None have been found, alive or deceased, which means they're either inside another bunker somewhere, or . . ."

"They cull the women." The words are halting, but I need to say them, if there's any chance of helping more women be rescued from the sadistic Cabal bastards. "That's what they called it.

Culling, like what farms do with breeder cows that don't produce anymore. So, when you stop responding to their treatment to produce eggs, do you think they just . . ." I can't bear to finish that sentence. Can't do it.

Glitch makes a strangled sound in his throat, and there are several other sounds of disgust and revulsion around the table.

Fletcher squeezes my knee, slowly running his thumb over the outside of my leg. I focus on the small comfort, hanging onto it like a lifeline, while I stare at the meaningless faux-wood pattern on the tabletop.

"There is obviously more here than meets the eye," Patrick says, his voice kind and tactful of the sensitive subject. "It sounds like, short of someone talking—which we're already working on—the next best thing would be to find and observe an active bunker. We've swept up enough information on their trucks, we can tighten up our search in that area. Perhaps it's as simple as them using the trucks to transport the genetic material to their main base, wherever that is."

"There is *no trace* of them being in contact with any other bunker. We know there *are* others. We've found two, and neither had records or an obvious contact method with the other. They designed these places to be silos. So even if we sweep one off, we can't cut the head off the dragon. And as much as I hate to admit it, I'm stumped. I've used every tool at my disposal, and I don't know where to look next." Glitch drops his head into his hands.

"Don't be so hard on yourself, buddy. This organization has been hiding for centuries. We'll crack them because we're not giving up," Atlas says.

"Nobody expects you to fix it in a day, Glitch," Peter adds from across the table. "That's not how investigations work, not even with the weight of the entire NAA police force. It takes time, and almost always more resources than we expect. Which is the next question—what else can we tap into? What resources aren't we thinking of?" Peter looks around at each of us, but I have nothing else to add.

Unless nausea helps, but somehow I think we all feel it.

"I have a friend I can call," Patrick says, rubbing his hand over the back of his neck as he shoots a weighty look at Nell and Atlas, then Glitch. "They're loath to work outside their own community. But I think given the circumstances, they'll help us. I'll make the call as soon as I'm on the plane."

The meeting breaks up after that, nothing more to be done for now except wait, and keep pushing for one of the Cabal to break, or a breakthrough on their technology.

But I'm already so tired of *waiting*.

The idea of an unknown number of more bunkers is horrifying. Once word gets out that I'm no longer in the bunker, are they going to come right back after me?

The possibility sends a chill through my veins that I just can't shake. I'm going down a very ugly mental rabbit hole when Peter walks over to me with a spring in his step.

"Demy, did Fletcher remember to give you my message? I've got something you're going to want." Peter's grin is infectious, the exact opposite of his solemnity just a moment before.

"He remembered, so don't maim him." I shoot a dramatic look at Fletcher, who just rolls his eyes in response.

"Only if you ask me to," Peter says with a wink. "Come on."

Chapter Thirty-Five

SHADOWS IN THE NIGHT

DEMY

I spend the next several hours hidden away in my room, alone with Peter's gift. I'd rather be outside, breathing the fresh air . . . but the reminder that we haven't caught *all* of the Cabal keeps me inside, hiding, despite my favorite bow, and a quiver slam full of shiny, deadly arrows that he brought along. They bring me a degree of comfort, just being on the side table next to me. He also brought me the rest of my weapons collection, including a new, stronger replacement taser for the one that got smashed when I was abducted.

But something is niggling at my memory, something that feels important, but I can't put my finger on it. My time inside is already starting to feel fragmented, certain pieces hard to grasp. Or maybe it's just plain old fear. Sometimes, it's hard to know the difference.

My room is nothing like my cell, at least. There's a TV, a comfortable bed with plenty of blankets and enough squishy pillows to build myself a fort out of.

Clean pillows that smell like laundry detergent.

I can walk out and get any food or drinks I want. Most importantly of all, there's no Lee or his wandering hands . . . I shut that thought down quickly.

Am I ever going to be free of the Cabal? If not the men themselves, the memories? I don't know, and it's a knife to the heart. A soft knock comes at my door, sometime in the afternoon. I skipped lunch because I didn't have an appetite. Apparently, being on two-meal-a-day rations for an extended period of time screws with your internal clock. Another parting gift from my time locked away.

"Who is it?" I ask, not bothering to extricate myself from my mound of pillows, or turn off the cooking show I'm watching.

Even though I have little to no skills of my own to speak of, it's the only genre of television that doesn't have something in it to set me off. Which is why I've been watching a perfectly coiffed woman whisk egg whites for what feels like ten straight minutes. Eggs have never personally offended, attacked, or imprisoned me.

Maybe I should become a chef.

There's no answer, just the soft creak of the door hinges as someone peeks in. When I look over and see Sherese, every muscle in my body locks down. I can't even say why; it's just instinct.

She must see me freeze up, because she pauses, waiting.

"Come in?" I say, not sure why it comes out as a question.

She does silently, letting the door stay cracked behind her. *I'm not the only one with trauma, here.* The reminder loosens up my lungs a little, and I can suck in a normal breath again. Sherese takes a desk chair without asking, leaving a few feet between us.

I'm starting to feel a little silly, with only my head and neck sticking up out of my pillow mound, but decide not to care.

We stare at each other for a long time, neither of us speaking. The chipper blonde cook has finished whisking, moving on to sifting a bunch of powders together, none of which I recognize the names of except flour. But I don't turn it off, because the noise is a difference. A constant reminder that I'm okay.

"Most of the women are gone, now," Sherese says, plucking at the hem of her black t-shirt. It's standard issue, loosely fitted, and she's got it paired with matching sweatpants. This is the only time I've ever seen her not wearing one of her brightly colored dresses. She seems smaller, somehow. Like a balloon that's lost some of its air overnight, which is an odd thought. "I'll be leaving in about an hour. I wanted to see you first."

"Well, you found me," I say. I'm not trying to be flippant, really. I just don't have words for this. Not yet. I fidget with the edge of the case on one of my pillows. What does she possibly have to say to me? We were in an awful place together, but we . . . were not actually friends, despite what I thought in the beginning.

We survived, but that was all. And my *personal* fight isn't over.

"They told us what happened that night. After we were all here, and changed and clean and fed. The woman in charge told us it was you."

I go still again, the pillowcase still clutched between my hot fingertips as understanding dawns.

"You saved us. You put yourself out there, and you saved *every single one of us.*"

"No, I didn't. The men were already close—"

She holds up a hand, cutting me off. Not that the words are exactly pouring out of me, but I'm trying, here.

"You *helped*. It could have been weeks longer, without what you did, or they might have stolen us right back out from under their noses. And I just wanted to say that I . . . I'm ashamed of myself."

Sherese's voice cracks, and panic threatens to choke me. I can barely deal with my *own* emotional soup right now. I don't know how to comfort her, not even a little bit.

She bites her knuckle, repressing a sob, then shakes her head before letting her hand drop back into her lap. "I mean it. I thought I was doing my best. It had been so long, Demy. I didn't think that getting out was possible. I really, truly believed that my life was over. And I hope you'll forgive me for letting that man hurt you, while I turned my back. But even if you do, I know I won't forgive myself for not having the courage to stand up."

I stare at the wall. I'm at a complete loss for words, and if I stare at the wall I won't see the tears roll down her cheeks. I won't see that I somehow broke this woman, this stoic survivor.

We sit in silence for a minute, maybe two. And then she stands up, near-silently, except the soft whisper of slipper-treads on the tile floors. She doesn't say anything else, just slides a large envelope onto the night stand next to me. But when I hear the creak of the door's hinges, I call out.

"Wait. Just—" I swallow hard, and force myself to look up at her. She's frozen in the doorway, a woman out of time. Proud and broken, regal and lost.

Human.

We're all just people.

"You helped me, too. Maybe not that night," I say, the words bitter on my tongue at the memory. "But if you hadn't encouraged me to befriend Lee, I never would have made it to the surface. I never could have left the message. So you helped, too."

She purses her lips, now refusing to meet my eyes. But I see the subtle answering nod, a single jerk of her chin, even though her body is turned almost completely away.

"Do you think surviving is enough?" Sherese asks, her back still turned my way, one foot out the door.

I think about it—really think about it—for a moment. The question matters.

"I think it has to be."

She nods one more time, and then she's gone. Out of the door, and out of my life.

I'm relieved to see her go, and a little terrified of what's in the envelope.

I distanced myself from the others, the longer I was inside the bunkers. I had Nell, I had myself, and after my connection with Sherese fizzled . . . I let myself be closed off. It was easier. *Safer.* But my fingers are drawn to it like magnets, and I bring it up in front of my nose. There's nothing on the outside, and my hands shake as I lift the flap.

There are only two sheets of paper inside, and I suck in a sharp breath when I see the first. A rainbow-hued drawing, in messy crayon. It's a little girl under the bright blue sky, holding a woman's hand. They're both smiling, standing in green grass, and there is a rainbow squished into one corner. A name is written in pen at the bottom corner, in tight, tidy script.

By Amelia.

The second sheet of paper is almost empty, a simple note in the same handwriting.

Demy,

Thank you. Not for myself, because I don't deserve my freedom, or your forgiveness. Not after I played a part in hurting other women. But for my Amelia . . . I was willing to do anything.

Thank you for setting her free.

—Annie

I close my eyes, tears streaming down my face as the dam bursts, the hard shell of indifference I built around my heart shattering into a million shards.

By the evening, my stomach has finally gotten the message that I should eat. I'm debating leaving the room, or picking up the phone they provided me to ask for an in-room meal, when a soft knock comes at the door.

I'm wary, after my last visitor, that another woman might have come to share a tearful goodbye. I don't feel like I saved anyone, so the idea of any more expressions of gratitude makes my stomach turn.

But it's Fletcher who pokes his head in, and with him comes the aroma of grilled beef and gooey cheese. My stomach lets out a rumble of approval.

"Hi," I murmur.

"Hey," he says with a smile. The look is full of warmth, and sends a slow, syrupy sweetness unfurling through me. Like lemonade on a hot summer's day, and all he said was one word.

"I don't know if you've already had dinner, but I was craving a cheeseburger. And the last one we had got interrupted, so I thought maybe you'd want one, too." He smiles, then holds up a red tray, massively over-laden with greasy food.

It looks *absolutely freaking amazing.*

I wave him in, subconsciously shoving some of my unkempt hair behind my ears as he sets the tray on the desk.

"Be right back," he says, kissing me on the forehead before jogging back out of the room. Less than two minutes later, he's back with colorful paper cups, straws sticking out of the tops with the paper still on. "Can't forget the lemonade." He grins, handing me one before settling in at the desk chair.

I take a sip, the flavor bursting on my tongue as he slides about a third of the food off the tray onto the table, and then carries the lion's share over to me.

"No pressure, you don't have to eat all of it or even any of it, if it doesn't sound good. The kitchen staff thought it was a bad idea, going so heavy after they had you on tight rations. But . . . I don't know. Sometimes what's good for you isn't what's *good for you,* you know?"

Our eyes lock together as our fingertips touch on the tray. It's a simple, innocent touch. A friendly gesture; food, comfort, companionship. But it feels like so much more.

"It smells better than anything I've had in a month," I say, taking the tray and squinching it down on top of a pillow. "Probably shouldn't eat it in bed, but—"

"You get a pass. Besides, the tray will catch most of the crumbs." He waves away the rules of normal food decency, already shoving a couple fries in his mouth.

I look at the tray, unsure what to eat first. There's a burger, as promised, gooey yellow cheese sliding down the side. Fries, of course. Onion rings, some weird blobby fried things I can't identify, a slice of cheesecake, and even a small bowl of salad, covered in fresh cherry tomatoes, bright red onions, and carrots.

I have a feeling *that* was from the kitchen staff, but it's still sweet. He covered all the bases. I pick up a fry, the crisp saltiness calling to me the most. It tastes like heaven, and that first bite has my eyes sliding closed in pure, unadulterated food bliss. I'm pretty sure I let out a moan, too, but I don't care. I quickly open my eyes, working my way around the tray and sampling all the things. I'm surprised to find corn inside the blobs, which are surprisingly addictive.

I look up a moment later to find him staring, french fries abandoned.

"What's wrong? Do I have cheese on my chin or something?" I ask, swiping self-consciously with a napkin.

"Nope, you're perfect. I've just never been jealous of a corn nugget before."

I snort-laugh at that, slapping my hand over my face in embarrassment. That gets a chuckle out of him, too, and then we're both giggling like children as we stuff our faces.

Once I've eaten until I'm bursting at the seams—which only takes a paltry amount of the food he brought me, I'm sad to say—he takes the tray and sets it outside the door, leaving his own trash on it as well.

He lingers at the door, indecision clear on his handsome face. "Thanks for letting me come by. I've been trying to give you space, but I just . . . I needed to make sure you were okay." He smiles, but his eyes are still tight.

He's holding back, trying not to overwhelm me.

Making a split-second decision, I pat the edge of the bed, inviting him to sit. He softly closes the door, and walks back to my side.

The bed dips under his weight, and I reach for his hand, twining our fingers together. I'm suddenly shy, even though absolutely nothing has changed.

It's a ridiculous feeling, like I've drunk too much fizzy soda and spun around on a carnival ride.

"Will you stay with me?" I ask, then quickly add, "Not to . . . do anything. Just to be here? I think that maybe I'm ready to not be alone." I risk a glance at his eyes and then quickly look away, embarrassed.

I trust him.

And it's not like it would be the first time we've spent an evening sleeping next to each other. But this time, there's no other man in the way. No weight of other people's feelings riding between us. Jax and Beckett are long gone, and unless something major changes . . . we might be spending *every* night together soon.

The idea feels comforting, but also momentous.

He hums a sound of approval, low in his throat. "I'll always be here when you need me, Demy. You know that, right?"

I bobble my head back and forth, not sure what to say to such a brave declaration. I'm taking baby steps, and he's *leaping* . . . further and faster than I can process. It's too much, and not enough. It's everything good, and also wholly overwhelming.

So, I bite my lip, and don't answer, staring like a coward at where our fingers are laced together on top of the fluffy white blankets.

His thumb grazes my lip, gently tugging it free of my teeth. "All that good food I just brought you, and still you're biting this beautiful lip," he teases, soothing the skin there gently. His gaze travels up from my mouth to my eyes and he says, "Yes, I will stay with you. No pressure. Just us."

I nod, tears welling up and threatening to spill at the kindness in his voice. I'm sure he notices—the man seems to notice *everything* about me, after all—but he doesn't make me feel bad. He just smooths a hand over my hair, kicks off his shoes, and climbs onto the other side of the bed.

A few minutes later, we've rearranged some pillows, turned down the lights, and I'm tucked under his chin. His chest is warm under my cheek, the steady thud of his heart comforting me on a deep, primal level. I drift off to sleep, secure for the first time in a long, long while, with the gentle weight of his hand on my back reminding me I'm not alone.

Chapter Thirty-Six

DECREE

Fletcher

"Fletcher?" Demy's uncertain voice jolts me out of sleep like a cattle prod.

I spring upright on the bed, ready to do battle with whatever has made her sound like that. "What is it? Get your bow."

She laughs lightly, and I turn to look down at her in confusion. I'm struck by how her hair is spread over the pillow like a dark silk curtain. "You've got an alarm or something going off." She gestures towards the desk, where I dropped my wrist comm last night.

"Crap, sorry." I shuffle off the end of the bed, and then mute it so I can read the message.

Royal Decree in seven minutes.

"Looks like there's an NAA-wide announcement," I murmur, showing her the glowing text.

"Oh! I bet the King and Queen—Sadie and Patrick? It's so weird to sort of know them and not know what to call them. But I bet she had the baby. I remember last time, they had a son and there was a big to-do." She grins sleepily up at me, hair a-tangle, and I want to thread my fingers into it and kiss her senseless, because she's the most beautiful sight I've ever woken up to.

But my teeth feel fuzzy, and I don't think she'd appreciate the morning breath.

"I bet they'll be watching it out in the main lobby. If we get dressed quickly, we can go see it with the gang," I offer.

I'd love to keep her to myself, of course. But I've noticed how she's tucked herself away, isolated, ever since her time in the Cabal's bunkers. A happy announcement . . . maybe it's a chance for a happy outing. Something to break the ice.

She grins ear to ear, nodding her approval and flicking off the covers. Before she can escape, though, I give into the urge to kiss her—chastely, on the forehead. She lets out the tiniest of contented sighs, and my heart soars even as I let her go so I can grab my things.

We both get cleaned up at light speed and I meet her at her door exactly six minutes later.

"Come on, we'll have to hurry. Where's the lobby?" she asks, grabbing my hand and looping our fingers together like it's as natural as breathing.

It nearly knocks me off my feet. I resist the urge to shake my head, try to focus. "Come on, not far." We half-jog through the halls, the squeaks of our tennis shoes on tile matching our upbeat moods. Her bow bounces on her shoulder with every stride, but I'm glad she has it. I want her to feel secure.

We careen around the last corner just as the royal anthem finishes playing. Sure enough, there's a single-camera video showing the royal crest on the big, full-wall display in the lobby of our temporary headquarters.

Most everyone is gathered, so Demy and I slip into the back, leaning against one of the black leather couches occupying the space. I keep her hand in mine, and watch as a second later, Patrick and Sadie appear on the screen.

A cheer goes up around the room.

"Look! She's got the baby!" someone shouts, pointing at the tiny, pink blanket bundle in Sadie's arms. Their other two children, Jacqueline and Zane are seated on small chairs, beaming up at the camera.

"Hello and welcome, friends, family, and all citizens of the North American Alliance," Patrick begins. "We've come together today to share the joyous news that our third child, the newest princess of the NAA, has been born. Sadie and I are absolutely thrilled to introduce you all to Penelope Faith Royce, born yesterday here at home. We would like to thank the doctor and midwife who attended, as well as each and every one of you for celebrating this occasion with us. Our hearts are truly full." He beams down at Sadie, pure love and devotion in his eyes.

A spark of jealousy flares, and I let go of Demy's hand just long enough to pull her against my side in a hug. The jealousy melts away instantly as she wraps her arms around me and squeezes me hard right back.

We might not be *there* yet—married with three kids—but the woman I love is safe, healthy, and at my side. I'll never get tired of that.

The rest will come in time. *When she's ready.*

"But that's not all we have to announce today."

Tense silence falls over the room. Demy looks up at me, worry in her eyes. I give her a small squeeze. I don't know what the announcement is, but after what we've been through the last few months . . . I'm not fazed. We'll figure it out.

"Our third child coming into the world has brought clarity, in a way that not much else can. Sadie and I have been discussing for years now the future of the NAA, and how we can all be stronger together. We have worked tirelessly, devoting ourselves wholly to that purpose. But there's one thing that's still missing. *Choice.*"

He stares deeply at the camera, and the hair stands up on the back of my neck. Choice? Does he mean . . .

"To honor the birth of our daughters, and all daughters of the NAA from here forward, we declare today to be Penelope Faith Abrogation Day. From today forward, the full scope of reproductive rights are returned to all female citizens of our great country. The Compulsory Marriage and Reproduction Act has been repealed, and is no longer enforceable in any tri-state or territory of the NAA. Official communications will be coming from our office with full details later this evening. Thank you, and good night."

The image zooms in for a moment on the picturesque family, the proud mother beaming at her husband, before it flickers back to the royal crest, and then to a shocked blonde reporter.

Whatever the reporter says, though, we don't hear. Because the cheers echoing off the walls of the lobby are so loud, it drowns everything out except the sounds of my own heartbeat in my ears.

Chapter Thirty-Seven

TROUBLE IN PARADISE

Demy

Shock. My ears are ringing with the cheers of elated people all around me, but all I can feel is shock. I look up at Fletcher and see the same reflected there.

Not joy, not excitement. *Shock.*

We don't have to get married. I'm free, and so is he. I should be elated. *Thrilled.* And on some level, I am. For women everywhere—no more forced marriages. No more mandatory babies before we're ready. It's . . . it's exactly the right thing to do. Noble, even, for someone in power to actually do what's right for a change.

So why do I feel numb? Like the rug's been pulled out from under me?

I back slowly away from Fletcher, letting my arm slip free from his waist. I need time to process. Space.

"Demy, don't. Please— I—"

I shake my head. I can't. He's looking at me, so intently, with all the color draining from his face, as if we're both processing in opposite directions. My mind is spinning forward, as fast as it can, and he's spinning away from me.

All the threads that tied us together, fraying to the breaking point in seconds.

I step back, putting another foot between us. He reaches out, his hand suspended in the air between us. The open palm, the thick calluses. The warmth I know I'd find if I slipped my hand into his.

But I can't.

I run. As fast as I can, I bolt out the front door. Footsteps pound after me. He's calling my name, but I don't pause at the automatic front doors. I run, and I run, as fast as I can.

My lungs burn, my side aches. But still, I don't stop.

Eventually he stops calling me. And when my legs turn to lead, when my breaths have been reduced to ragged sobs, only then do I let myself stop, collapse against the trunk of a tree.

The rough bark bites into me as I sag against it, the exposed skin of my shoulders snagging painfully against the bumpy, poking trunk as I slide down to a crouch. I pull my quiver and bow off my back, draping them over my knees.

Soft footsteps reach me before I'm even settled, making me whip my head up.

"It's just me," Fletcher says, his voice half hoarse. He's got his hands raised and chooses a tree a dozen feet away to lean against.

I want to rage, to scream, to send him away. But he looks so heartbroken that I can't. He's not making eye contact, despite following me on a wild chase through the woods.

I should have known he would. The man followed me to hell and dragged me out of the Cabal's clutches; I don't expect any less at this point.

Do I?

Everything about our lives just changed in one instant. It's like an earthquake, or a bomb going off. One moment, you're sitting at your kitchen table having breakfast. Everything is fine; not perfect, but fine. *Comfortable.* And then a massive force rips the ground apart underneath you, and everywhere you look something's broken. Shattered picture frames on the floor, doors hanging out of joint. Furniture toppled, splintered. Your ears are ringing.

That's what Patrick just did to us. To our relationship.

I suck the pine-scented air in through my nose, grateful for the crisp temperature, even as the cold burns my lungs.

"Nothing has to change between us," Fletcher says. The words are soft and low, meant to soothe and not to spook me.

So why are they like barbs in my soul?

"Everything's changed. *Everything*," I disagree. I finally meet his eyes, see the sadness there.

"Are you telling me that we're off? You're walking away?" He doesn't flinch, doesn't look away. But there's tension in every line of his body as he steps away from the tree to pace. The slope of his shoulders is sharp. The side of his neck looks carved from stone.

"I don't know."

His eyes sink shut, covering the chocolate depths. That little window into him, his inner fire, that I love so much.

Should I? Am I crazy?

"Don't walk away, Demy. Don't do that." His eyes spring back open, a fierce determination in their depths. He crosses the space between us in a few powerful strides, dropping to his knees in front of me. The scent of pine needles crushing will be forever branded into my mind, right along with the devastated look of him.

I don't want to devastate him. But I can't act like nothing's changed.

"I'm not the same person I was a month ago," I whisper. "Even before the announcement, I wasn't the same. It doesn't seem fair to tie you to me, under an obligation that no longer exists. You could go have a baby with any woman. You're so handsome, Fletch. So good." I reach up and trail my fingertips along his cheekbone. His warm, russet skin so alive and perfect beneath my fingertips. "You'll have your pick of women lining up to take a chance with you. Like Cammie."

He jerks back from my touch, even as the memory leaves a bitter taste in my mouth. Even now, something inside me is pulling me not to give him that leeway. But I'm wrong *not to*. He deserves better than me. A broken experiment of a woman. I'm just going to keep getting chased.

"Why do you think I would choose anyone else? What have I done so *wrong* that you still don't believe I'm here for you!" He rakes a hand through his hair, sending his bun askew.

"I've done everything—*everything!*—because I love you, Demy. Not the idea of you. Not the perfect picture in the Bachelorette Book, or the woman I met in a stunning feather-covered gown that first night. The real you. The you who eats cheeseburgers and talks about dreams, who exercises and wants to get married in a pair of stretch pants. The woman who's so strong, who's overcome every single thing life has thrown at her. *That's* the woman I love. So don't tell me I can have whoever I want. Because if I can't have you, then I can't have my pick. Because *you are my pick*."

He shoves off the ground, scattering leaves and pine needles everywhere. I watch as they fall slowly to the ground, because I can't bring myself to watch him walk away.

It's for the best.

It has to be. Because if I don't send him away? The Cabal will keep coming, keep hunting, and he'll end up like everyone else I've ever let myself love.

Dead.

CHAPTER THIRTY-EIGHT

VENGEANCE

DEMY

After each bout of fitful sleep tonight, I've awakened, completely alone, and reached over to touch my bow and finger the fletching on one of the arrows, just to make sure they're still there.

It's nothing like last night, when I slept the sleep of the beloved in Fletcher's arms. Safe and warm, tucked into his side like a cherished woman. But I can't have that tonight, and no matter how many times I toss and turn, he's not coming back. I won't let him.

I should want him to move on. The thought pounds against the inside of my skull like a tattoo. I should want him to. So why am I so low?

Because what you want and what you should want are two very different things. My inner monologue has taken on Nell's sass, and I can practically see her standing there, hand on her hip as she says it.

I refuse to acknowledge the point, even inside my own head. Being with me puts Fletcher in danger, and now . . . he doesn't have to be with me. I could accept it when he had no other choice for a baby. A family. Some part of me clung to that, the *necessity* of it all. But that's gone now.

And with it, my sleep.

I roll over, punching my pillow into submission with a sigh.

I'm staring at the ceiling when the ever-present hum of the ventilation system switches off. It takes me a moment to place the sudden absence, but when I do, all the little hairs on my arms stand up. I've been here for days now, and not once in that time has it shut off.

Until now.

My hand is on my bow and my feet are in my shoes before I consciously think about the motion. My pulse is pounding in my ears, a rapid drumbeat of blood racing through my veins. I stand for a moment, just waiting inside the door, feeling like a paranoid fool.

It's probably nothing.

This building is *full* of highly trained police, in addition to a chunk of Atlas's security team. Whoever's on guard will take care of any problems, assuming the building hasn't just . . . finally gotten to the perfect temperature, or something.

Which it probably has.

I drum on the grip of my bow, indecision warring with anxiety inside. What's the harm? If it's nothing, I'll walk around, see that it's nothing, and go back to bed. Maybe the walk will do me some good . . . and if it takes me past Fletcher's room—

No, I won't let myself go there.

I'm not running back to him in the middle of the night. We both need time to think. Process. I haven't *stopped* thinking about what he said.

Don't tell me I can have whoever I want. Because if I can't have you, then I can't have my pick. Because you are my pick.

The words spur me into action; anything to get away from the memory of his pained expression, and the deep knowledge that it's all my fault. But I'd rather cause him minor pain now than cost him his life somewhere down the line.

I shove open my bedroom door, stepping quietly into the dim hall. I'm enveloped by near-blackness. There are small emergency lights lit along the floor every few feet, but other than that and the distant red glow of an Exit sign at the end of the long hallway, nothing breaks the darkness. This is getting stranger and stranger, so I feel a little less silly for checking.

I walk quietly, bow relaxed but firm in my grip, quiver a comforting weight on my back. After I pass through two hallways and find nothing but more darkness, the knot between my shoulder blades starts to loosen. I'm standing at the corner of the halls that would take me to Fletcher's room, desire and frustration nearly eating me up inside.

This is ridiculous. Walk by and check that he's okay and go back to bed.

Huffing out a breath, I walk more quickly toward his room. I'm three doors down when I hear it. *Another set of footsteps.* I freeze, except for the hand that flies back to my quiver and draws an arrow. Everything slows down, as my eyes narrow on the corner, where the footsteps are coming from.

They're heavy, most likely a man in a pair of boots, and moving slowly.

Too slowly for a patrol. This guy is creeping.

I nock the arrow, and lift the bow, stepping closer to one of the closed doors lining the hall. It's not much but blending into the frame's shadow is my best option for not being seen immediately.

My palms are damp and my arms are shaking, even though there's no tension on the draw yet. It could be a patrol, or someone else with a wicked case of insomnia. I don't want to accidentally shoot an NAA officer, or one of Atlas's men.

A bead of sweat rolls down the back of my neck as the first outline of the person comes around the corner. It's a man, as I suspected.

It's dark, so I hold my breath and pore over the figure. Three things become abundantly clear in the next heartbeat; he's wearing a black cloak, his head is shaved bald, and when his eyes scan the hallway, they hold a familiar, icy menace.

The hiss of my string extending is his only warning, and he hears it. But the twang of my arrow's release is less than a blink later, and he doesn't see the shot coming in the unlit hallway. The bones in my hand scream at the motion, but I don't even register the pain. I'm so focused, so locked in on the man in the black cloak that nothing else matters.

He swears, the angry exclamation ending in a disgusting gurgle as he collapses to the ground with a deafening thud in the hallway. I keep my eyes peeled, dragging out another arrow, but rooted to the spot like a rabbit hiding from a fox.

A sickening sound comes from his collapsed form, and I resist the urge to close my eyes. But then an emergency alarm—almost like a tornado siren—is blaring throughout the building, and the overhead lights all come on at once. As soon as they do, I can see that he's down, my arrow sticking out of his neck. Blood is pooling beneath him, slowly widening into a lake on the floor.

The sight is sickening, and yet I can't drag my eyes away. He might get back up, might attack me, might choke me again—

Doors start flying open along both sides of the hall, confused and bleary-eyed people barging out into the hallway.

I can't move, though. I'm stuck to the spot like glue, even as horror fills me. Until Fletcher flies out of his room, sheer panic painted on his face, hair a wild halo of dense curls around his head.

He spots me immediately and panic turns to concern as he takes in my bow and whips his head toward the direction it's pointed.

"Cabal!" he yells, raising the alarm as he points to the fallen man.

I should have done that.

But I can't move, can't speak. I'm a scared little rabbit, always on the run.

It's already happening.

Fletcher is at my side in an instant, the other men in the hall surrounding the one I shot, all talking at once. I can only hear them in between the bleats of the tornado siren. Arms come around me, even as I hold a second, shaking arrow to the corner of my lips. My fingertips are wet from my tears, but I don't dare to dash them away.

Lee came back for me.

Lee escaped, and he came back for me.

"Demy, don't shoot. Demy!" Fletcher pushes the tip of the arrow down, lowering my bow towards the shiny, unthreatening tiles. I carefully release the string and let the arrow clatter to the floor. My fingers are hot and numb at the same time. The coppery tang of blood loud in my nose. His arms go around me in a second, crushing me to his chest in a hug.

"You're okay, it's all okay. You got him. You got him," he soothes me, rubbing circles on my back. More and more people pour into the hallway, making me feel claustrophobic. When Atlas's booming voice breaks over the crowd, Fletcher tugs me down to his own door, kicking it open with a sock-clad foot and ushering me inside.

As soon as it shuts behind us, a measure of calm comes over me.

"Are you okay? Did he hurt you?" Fletcher's earnest question breaks my bubble of shock.

"No, I'm fine— He . . . he'd only just come around the corner. I recognized him." I swallow hard, staring at our feet. Mine look oddly overdressed in black boots on the white tiles, while he's standing next to me in socks. It's an absurd thing to be thinking, which means that shock must still have its claws in me.

What's absurd is that I just shot a man. I killed someone.

"Demy!" He lifts my chin, searching my eyes. He's clearly worried, which is understandable.

"I'm sorry," I murmur, unsure what I missed; what he asked or said . . .

"Don't apologize to me. Don't— You're just scaring me. It's not your fault. It's all going to be okay." I reach for him, arms moving on autopilot, despite everything that's transpired between us in the last twenty-four hours.

He pulls me to his chest and then sinks onto the bed, settling me into his lap. A measure of calm returns, like he's my anchor in the tempest that is my life. The incessant attack.

We sit in silence until a knock comes, but I close my eyes like a coward and tuck my face into his chest when he calls for the person to come in.

"There was a Cabal attack on the prisoner holding area. A few were let out of their cells, but we've got air support rounding

228

them up now, and we've caught more than we started with. Two of them apparently missed the company line about getting out of Dodge and back to cockroach central, because he and his buddy cut the power to the building and tampered with the emergency backup power system. It triggered Glitch's alarms, but it took a few minutes to override and get the power back on."

Two of them. And I shot—

"What about the man in the hallway?"

"Dead. Not sure which one he is." Atlas's voice is impassive, but I can't help but flinch against Fletcher's grip.

"It was Lee," I whisper. Fletcher tightens his arms around me, all the while careful to keep his fingertips gentle on the back of my neck.

"Lee?" Fletcher's voice is tight with the question. Strained.

"The one I was with when you found me," I clarify.

"Good," he says, the word more snarl than anything.

"Good?" I ask, finally looking up in surprise.

"*Good.* That SOB had it coming for what he did to you. I'd have done it myself, if the police hadn't swooped in." His eyes drop from mine to my throat and back. I know exactly what he's remembering; the ring of fingerprint-shaped bruises. The cracks in my bones. The demand to strip off my dress on a dirty mattress.

I let my eyes close again, and he tucks me under his chin.

Safe, I'm safe now.

"I'll let Glitch know it was personal, and the man's name. See if there's anything else we can glean from this incident . . ." He clears his throat. "The other was Lars. The man who kidnapped you from the NLC."

Every muscle in my body tenses in reflexive terror. His hawklike eyes are burned into my brain. The way he befriended me, only to betray me in the worst way possible.

"Did he get away?" I whisper, scared to know, but more afraid not to.

At that, a half grin spreads across Atlas's face. "Why, no, he didn't. He happened to be in my hallway when the alarms went off. I was forced to subdue him, much like you subdued Lee." He holds my stare, letting those words sink in.

Lee is gone. Lars is gone. Neither one of them is going to hurt me, ever again. The Cabal might be out there, but my two personal tormentors? They're gone.

I shudder, Fletcher's shirt gripped tightly in my fist as the wave of emotion works its way through my body.

"Thank you, Atlas," Fletcher says as he holds me, his hands gentle, yet unwavering. *Steady.*

He nods, but hesitates in the doorway. "We'll move you out in the morning, Demy. A new safe house, a new start—where you'll stay until we've finished sweeping up every last one of them. Somewhere they won't find you. You will be safe. You have my word." Atlas's tone bears a heavy weight of regret, and the click of the door behind him has a finality to it that sinks into my stomach like a lead weight.

"Tomorrow," Fletcher says, his voice gone dull.

I don't have any words, so I say nothing. I just keep my eyes clenched shut. If I don't open them, I won't see Lee coming back for me.

Again, and again, and again.

CHAPTER THIRTY-NINE

ACTION

DEMY

Fletcher kept me tucked up in his bed all night. He didn't press while we cuddled, though I could feel the question hanging in the air between us. Was he coming with me? Would I let him?

A soft knock at the door wakes us around seven, and I open it to find a package of clothing. *My clothing.* The beautiful, soft, exercise gear I love so much from the NLC brings tears to my eyes, and I spin to Fletcher with what I'm sure is a dopey look on my face.

"Oh, good, they finally got it here!" He grins ear to ear, and I still.

"You knew?"

"Of course. Who do you think asked them for it?" He softly runs his thumb along my jaw, sending sparks flying through me—sparks I'm wholly unprepared for.

Have I been prepared for anything since stepping foot on that stupid bus? Not a dang thing. And yet somehow . . . I'm standing here with a gorgeous, kind, thoughtful man. Who listens, who cares.

Who loves me.

And I keep pushing him away, like he's not the best thing to come out of my messed up wreck of a life. I toss the pair of pants I was cuddling onto the bed, and something in my expression clues him into my thoughts, because he takes a half step forward, closing the last bit of distance left between us. His hands are on my upper arms, lightly, not boxing me in. *Soaking* me in. And it's delicious.

"Demy?" he asks, as if unsure what's changed all of a sudden.

But for the first time, I'm crystal freaking clear.

I press up onto my toes, weave my fingers into his long, soft curls, and pull his lips down to mine. No tiptoeing around, no hesitant touches. All want, and heat, and passion. His lips are soft on mine, but as soon as I give the green light by starting the kiss, he takes it up a notch.

His hands are around my waist in a flash, anchoring us together as he devours me, slanting his lips across mine in a haze of need.

Everything narrows, until there's no one and nothing but the two of us. One of his warm hands on my back, the other cupping the back of my neck. His silken hair under my fingertips, his solid chest under my other hand—so opposite to me, and so exciting at the same time.

I'm utterly breathless by the time his lips leave mine, trailing kisses across my cheek, down my jaw. Every touch is new, lighting me up inside and making me want so much more. *Everything. I want everything.*

His wrist comm buzzes, freezing us in our tracks. I feel his low groan in the pit of my stomach.

"We could ignore it," he murmurs against my neck, silencing the sound without looking.

It immediately starts up again, and I can't help but laugh at the awful timing. I put my hands on his shoulders—when did he sink into the desk chair? I didn't notice, but I take advantage, sitting myself sideways across his lap and dropping my head to his shoulder.

"What does it say?" I prod when he doesn't move to check it.

"Emergency debriefing, of course," he says. He drops his lips to the top of my hair with a resigned sigh, wrapping his arms tightly around me in a bear hug, as if I'm going to disappear into mist if he lets me go.

We share one more soft, tender kiss, and then stand up to head to the meeting—but not until *after* I change into my favorite pants.

Despite the interruption, my heart is full, and there's a warm glow in my belly that I've never felt before. We still have so much to talk about, so much to work through. I'm still afraid, and that may never go away. At least not until the Cabal is dealt with . . . but something inside me has shifted.

The debriefing room is standing room only, and there are a few new faces. Mav's back; Atlas's right-hand man Easton, too; and someone's already got a big wall display cranked up, with Sadie and Patrick sitting in attendance. She's got a blanket tossed over her shoulder, and appears to be nursing the newest little princess Penelope underneath.

She looks tired, but happy in a way that I envy. Will I ever be that secure?

I don't need or want to be queen. But . . . to be so thoroughly loved, so thoroughly happy? Safe to bring a baby into this world? I cast a quick glance at Fletcher on reflex.

There's only one way to find out.

Nell waves me over to a free seat next to her, an excited grin on her face. As soon as I sink into it she looks me up and down frankly.

"Well, look who's back to herself. And that's quite a *glow* you're sporting this morning," she teases, before leaning in conspiratorially. "Or is it beard burn?" she adds in a whisper.

I flush from the roots of my hair to the base of my neck, embarrassment flooding me as I shove her playfully away.

"Demy and Fletcher, sitting in a tree—" she sing-songs, but blessedly lets it end there, as Atlas clears his throat and stands on her other side. Fletcher squeezes my shoulder, so I look up and he gives me a cheeky wink, not even a *bit* embarrassed at being called out by Nell.

No, he just looks happy.

"Thank you all for coming. This will be our last briefing here. As you all know, last night there was a rescue attempt staged by the Cabal to retrieve their men. I'm happy to report that it was largely unsuccessful, with all but two of our original captives accounted for. But in total, we've swept up an additional twenty-three men—those who staged the breakout. Their mistake cost them, and we're going to continue pressing the advantage."

Applause goes up around the room, even as my mind goes back to the huddled lump that used to be Lee, lying in a pool of his own blood in the hallway, with my arrow sticking out of him.

The image will probably stick with me for the rest of my days. The horror and relief of that moment weigh in equal measure.

But I can't regret it, not after the horrors the Cabal has inflicted on me, on my own parents. Treating women like disposable trash, to be used, abused, and thrown out when we're no longer productive or pliant.

Rage builds behind my breastbone. I don't want to celebrate. I don't want to hide, or cower, or pull back. I want to *destroy them.* Every single man, every single abusive doctor. I want to dismantle everything they've so proudly built in the dark. Drag it into the light of day and make sure there's no nook, no cranny, no crevice so small they can find another foothold in, ever.

Atlas holds up a hand for silence. "I want to say thank you to our newest arrivals for joining the hunt and introduce you all to Lilah." He gestures to a stunning Black woman, maybe in her early twenties, standing next to Mav. She's wearing a beautifully dyed, floor-length dress in a bright wash of colors. Her hair is in shoulder-length two-strand twists, with a top knot and beautiful silver beads interspersed throughout.

Lilah waves enthusiastically at the group, taking the time to make eye contact with each of us as she glances around. She's got a woven bag slung over her shoulder, and a heavy-duty-looking tablet clutched in her other hand.

"Lilah is a tech specialist, sent by a friend of Patrick's." He glances at Patrick, who nods once at the statement, but offers nothing more.

So secretive. I wonder where she came from?

"She's been working with Glitch for the two hours since they arrived, and they've already made some discoveries after last night's attack."

"We just missed all the action, apparently," Lilah says, her voice softly lilting with an accent I can't place.

"Hush, girl. Action is never good," Mav scolds with a shake of her head. "These young pups don' *know.*" She shoots Patrick a long-suffering look.

Lilah looks a little chastised, but too excited to take the scolding more than surface deep.

"Glitch, Lilah? Who wants to present your findings?" Atlas asks.

I look over at Glitch for the first time when he doesn't immediately launch into a ramble, and . . . is he blushing? I bite back a grin at the usually talkative man's uncharacteristic silence.

He is so crushing on Lilah. I share a quick glance with Nell, whose eyes are wide with glee, clearly having realized the same thing I have.

"I can share," Lilah offers, completely unaware that she's struck Glitch dumb with her effortless beauty. "The radios your team recovered were equipped with some tech we haven't found inside any of the bunkers themselves. It appears that their transport vehicles do more than just blend in. They're mobile comms centers, the only true connection between their bases. Most have simple radio systems, but one seems to act as the command center, which we were able to tap into." She pauses, looking at Glitch to see if he has anything to add.

He waves for her to continue, fiddling with the side cover of his own tablet.

"Greg's programming combined with our superior tech"—she waves her oversized tablet while I'm putting together that Glitch's real name is apparently *Greg* and nobody told me—"was able to trace back through their networks quite efficiently, and we've identified seven more signatures that we believe to be bunkers inside the NAA."

Seven more bunkers. We've got them. The idea of so many more is as horrible as hopeful. Every bunker we *know* exists is one that gets wiped off the map. I reach up and grip Fletcher's hand where it rests on my shoulder, and he squeezes me back.

"Are you sure you don't want to explain the rest, Greg? I'm less familiar with your political structure, so I might miss something." She tucks a lock of hair behind her ear, seeming uncertain for the first time as she meets his eyes.

"Uh, sure. Sorry," he stammers, pushing hurriedly to his feet. "As Lilah so eloquently established, there are at least seven bunker signatures remaining inside the NAA. She was able to map nine total pings, and we then used the information we had on the two current bunkers to identify rough locations for seven new bunkers we didn't previously know about. Together we analyzed the data, and found crime clusters in each of the tri-states where the signatures are located, giving further credibility to the locations. However, that is not the most important bit. We found one communication line that was different from the rest."

He taps his tablet a few times, and the wall display splits, Sadie and Patrick shrinking into half, while a world map pops up on the rest of the display. "Can you guys see that remote?" he asks.

"Yes, we can, thank you Glitch," Sadie says with a smile, patting Penelope's little bum.

"Okay. Well, these are the nine bunker locations." Nine red dots pop up on the NAA map like angry pimples, though two are faded slightly—the ones we've already cleared. The other seven are widely dispersed, from Nunavland Territories up north all the way down to this one, in New Texas. "And this is the communications base we found contact with." He taps again, a dotted red line swooping across the ocean, and landing dead center of the Collected European Republic, where a new angry red dot appeared.

"Oh, shi—" I clamp a hand down on Nell's arm as she swears.

"Ahh, yeah . . ." Glitch nodded at Nell's blunt assessment. "This was both unexpected, and extremely concerning. Further digging

237

is necessary, but our initial assessment is that the Cabal has ties to the CER, and more than that . . . we believe it's likely that the CER might actually be pulling the strings."

A silent pall descends on the room, as all eyes swivel to Patrick and Sadie, our regents. If the Cabal is being directed by the CER, that's not just bad news for us, that could be *war*. Goosebumps rise on my arms, and I clutch Fletcher's fingers more tightly as we all process this new bomb that just got dropped in our laps.

"Thank you, Glitch and Lilah"—he nods to both of them in turn—"for your excellent work. This is an incredibly disturbing discovery, and one we will absolutely need to get to the bottom of. Please continue digging, and let me know if you need additional crown resources to deal with any international roadblocks you may encounter. If the Cabal is being run or manipulated by the CER in any fashion, big or small, we're going to need to assemble a delegation to go and deal with this, immediately."

"Actually," Lilah interjects, holding up a finger tentatively, and Patrick waves for her to continue. "You might have a way to get there without raising suspicions. The Decennial International Fertility Summit is in less than a month. Every organized nation is invited to bring a delegation, and your formal invites should be arriving any day now. Perhaps your delegation just looks a little . . . *different* this time than ten years ago." She waves around the room, encompassing all of us.

"Perhaps it does," Patrick agrees, a look of weariness on his face as he looks over at Sadie, and down at their brand new baby. "We'll need time to plan and speak with our international advisors, but please keep us apprised of anything else you learn."

"Of course, Patrick," Glitch says with a solemn nod. The screen winks out, taking the ominous map away with our rulers.

CHAPTER FORTY

A QUESTION

DEMY

An hour later, a friendly aide named Sarah knocks on my door, letting me know that my safe house transportation has arrived. I'm surprised that Fletcher isn't with her, and a little confused. My things, besides my bow and quiver on my back, are all packed up in the simple duffle that arrived with my clothes this morning. My picture from Amelia is carefully tucked on top, so it doesn't get wrinkled. If I never do anything else good in my life, I will treasure that joyful picture, and the little girl who made it. I step out of the room, following the aide down the hall to the front foyer.

Where is Fletcher? He was supposed to be packing, too.

Unless he changed his mind? The news about the Cabal, the CER, the possibility of *war* made him realize what I was really wound up in?

Dread and fear curdle in my stomach like sour milk as we arrive at the *very empty* foyer.

Fletcher and I haven't spoken about concrete plans beyond moving to the safe house today, but after the kiss this morning, it seemed like we were on the same page, about continuing to explore our relationship.

But as the aide and I walk out the front sliding glass doors to see a waiting bus like the one that delivered me to the NLC the first time, my heart sinks into my feet.

He's not here. I stop beside the bus, turning to look at Sarah. "Sarah, have you heard—"

The glass doors slide open again, and I look up with relief to see Fletcher, running with a bag on his shoulder, and something clutched under his arm.

"Sorry! Don't leave without me!" He slides to a stop next to me with a huff, breathing hard like he's been running for a while. "I had to swing by the command room to get something from Glitch, but he was tied up with the whole European thing, and he'd forgotten—understandable, I know—but then he had to dig it out for me, and then I was late." He pins me with a brilliant smile, and all the fear leaves me.

He wasn't standing me up. We're still okay, for now.

I can breathe again.

Sarah chuckles, patting him on the shoulder. "We weren't going to leave without you, Fletcher. You're on the transport list." She shakes her head, then waves a goodbye. "You two have a lovely trip." She heads for the door, leaving just me and Fletcher, alone on the pavement.

He drops his own duffel bag with a thud, and suddenly I'm nervous for a different reason.

"What did you have to get from Glitch? Err, are we supposed to call him Greg, now? That just seems weird, after knowing him as Glitch for so long." My brain is spiraling. Nerves, relief, and back again give me whiplash as I stare at Fletcher, who's looking at me funny.

No, not funny, *intently.*

And why did he drop his bag?

"Should we go around and get on, or—"

"Demy, you know I love you, right?" He asks, searching my face.

"I— Yes, you've said it a few times now." Worry creeps up the back of my neck. Is he having second thoughts *now*?

"I know I've said it, but do you *know*? Really, in here?" He taps my chest, right over my heart. "Because I love you so much it feels like nothing is right when you're not around. Having you taken from me was the most painful experience of my life, and we'd only just met. I can only imagine how badly it hurt for you to have your parents taken as a kid. How it's shaped you, and your sense of security. And I know it's fast. I know I'm too much sometimes. But I can't stop loving you. *Wanting* you, and wanting to be with you."

He rakes a hand through his hair, and then holds up the object under his arm. It's a laptop, thin and shiny and expensive looking. "This is for you. It's loaded with everything you need to get your diploma remotely. I don't know how long we'll be at the safe house, but I knew it was important to you before, and that got derailed with everything that's happened. But I hear you, Demy, and I *see you.* All of you. The good, the bad, and I won't say ugly, because as far as I'm concerned, you're the most beautiful woman on the planet. But I love all the pieces of you, even the ones you try to hide."

My knees go weak and tears spring into my eyes at the words, even though it's cliché. But he doesn't hand me the laptop. He sets it carefully on the duffel bag, then looks back up at me.

I suck in a nervous breath as he keeps talking.

"We have no idea what comes next; you know that, and I know that. But there's one thing that's been a constant for me since all of this started. *You.* My feelings for you, the desire for more. Our friendship, and the connection that keeps growing despite everything that's been thrown at us. My love. When you were gone, I couldn't sleep, couldn't eat, couldn't *think* about anything except getting you back. Making you mine. Loving you, for the rest of our lives. And I don't want to take another step, down whichever road we're heading, without laying it all out on the line."

There's hope in his expression, as well as a healthy dose of fear as he sinks to one knee, right there in the headquarters parking lot, next to the waiting bus.

"Demelza Carlisle, you're the love of my life, and the most incredible woman I've ever met. The fire inside you inspires my days, and lights up my nights. Will you make me the happiest man on the planet, and be my wife?"

Oh my God. Ohmygod, ohmygod.

"I—"

Thank you so much for reading Captive! This book was a roller coaster to write, and it's going to stick with me for a long time. I feel like I went on this journey with Demy, and it left me wrung out more than once. But I can't stop rooting for our brave runaway, no matter how bad things get.

The story isn't over yet, and Valiant is shaping up to be every bit as wild a ride.

You can pre-order it here if you want to have it delivered to your kindle as soon as it's ready!

Want more of Nell & Atlas? Click here for an exclusive bonus scene.

Or, in the meantime, catch up on one of my other complete trilogies:

Endless Desert

Populations Crumble

Chapter Forty-One

DELETED SCENE – ALTERNATE "DECREE" BEGINNING

Just for Fun!

Waking up next to Demy is a dream. At first, I think it's literally a dream—my sleep has been fraught since she was taken. But today, the dream gives way to warm, soft reality. She's snuggled up under my chin, her soft breaths in and out, deep and even in sleep.

I can't help it, gratitude that this *isn't* a dream has me squeezing her just a little bit tighter. She murmurs something soft and sleepy, so I let her go again.

She tries again. "Fletcher?"

"Hmm?"

"What's that noise?"

I blink, staring up at the ceiling in the dark. She's right, there is a noise.

Beep beep. Beep beep.

Shoot. I took off my wrist comm when we lay down the night before.

"Sorry, I'll get it."

"M'kay." She pats me on the arm, not moving as I attempt to extricate myself to pick up the offending comm.

"Ah, looks like there's another debrief this morning. It starts in fifteen minutes. Do you want to get moving?" I ask, looking back over at her.

She rolled right over into the warm depression I left behind, snoring lightly—though I'd never tell her that—in the middle of her halo of dark curls. I chuckle at the sight, taking a mental snapshot.

I don't want to leave her, though, so I try again.

"Demy," I shake her shoulder lightly.

She swats my hand away.

"We have a meeting. Come on . . . We can get breakfast first if we hurry."

Demy pulls the pillow over her head, making a rude gesture with one hand in the process. I snort a laugh.

"Final offer. If you get up and get changed, I'll bring you coffee before we go."

"Fine, but I'm not going to be happy about it."

"I can live with that," I say with a laugh. Once I'm up, I'm up for the day. So in five minutes flat, I'm already down the hall to my room, dressed in fresh clothes, and cleaned up for the morning. Another five and I've got the coffees, and am nearly back to her room.

The light is on under the door at least, so I tap lightly to let her know I'm back, not wanting to startle her.

"Come in," she grouses.

CHAPTER FORTY-TWO
PLAYLIST

G litch by Taylor Swift

Bring it Back by Shawn Mendes

Rock and a Hard Place by Bailey Zimmerman

I'm Not Alright by Shinedown

I'll Follow You by Shinedown

Burning House by Cam

Wreckage by Nate Smith

A Symptom of Being Human by Shinedown

Carry on Wayward Son by Kansas

AND

Carry on Wayward Son by NEONI

. . . They're both good, y'all.

BEFORE YOU GO . . .

Thank you so much for reading Captive! I hope you enjoyed it and are looking forward to Valiant as much as I am. If you'd like an easy link to pre-order, you can scan this code:

Your taking the time to leave a review means the world to me and helps encourage more people to pick up the book and give it a chance. If you would take a moment to leave a rating or review before you go on to your next read, I would be so thankful. I read each and every one, and keep your kind words close on those days it's hard to keep writing.

If you would like to get a little bit more of Atlas and Nell, I have a free bonus scene available exclusively to my newsletter subscribers, which you can get by signing up here:

I post regularly on Facebook and Instagram as @kagandyauthor, and I am available by email at kagandyauthor@gmail.com as well, if you'd ever like to drop me a line directly! I love to hear from my readers!

MORE BY K. A. GANDY

<u>Post-Apocalyptic Adventure</u>

In The Dust

Finding the Bastion

Descendants of Rust

<u>Dystopian Romance</u>

Dwindle (Populations Crumble, Book 1)

Rise (Populations Crumble, Book 2)

Reign (Populations Crumble, Book 3)

Marked(Populations Crumble: Resurgence, Book 1)

Captive (Populations Crumble: Resurgence, Book 2)

Valiant (Populations Crumble: Resurgence, Book 3)
Fantasy

Aerthen Sight (An'Loran Chronicles, FREE Prequel Short)

The Lost Talisman(An'Loran Chronicles, Book 1)
The Hatchling – Coming Soon! (An'Loran Chronicles, Book 2)

About the Author

K. A. Gandy was born and raised in Jacksonville, Florida, and is married with two kids. She has worked as a restaurant hostess, library book shelver, ranch hand, tour guide, Realtor, tech whiz, landlord, and small business consultant, all in addition to pursuing her passion of writing. She likes to write late in the evenings and thinks drinking hot tea and baking great cookies fuels hopes and dreams.

If you would like to find more of her works, you can sign up for her newsletter here.

You can also get updates by following her on on Facebook, Instagram, or Tiktok @kagandyauthor.